## Sudde... Came To Life

With a start, Josh realized that the petite woman who was dressing the window had become such a part of the total picture that it was unnerving to see her move. He watched along with the passersby, absorbed in the magic she was creating.

Her movements in the confines of the window were sure and graceful, and her face was a study in concentration as she perfected the scene.

Josh stood rooted for a moment after the woman had gathered her supplies and left the window. Her high cheekbones would have been the envy of many a model. The point was that somehow this human dynamo had created interest in his store. As they'd walked away, the people had been discussing his store, his fashion image, his merchandise and prices.

Josh considered going directly to the display department and promoting this young lady to something akin to chairperson of the board but decided such a move would be completely out of character. Joshua Carrington rarely acted against his own, highly disciplined principles. His mind returned to the woman in the window. He found himself replaying the details of her appearance, her manner.

She had captivated everyone watching her—including him.

Dear Reader:

Series and Spin-offs! Connecting characters and intriguing interconnections to make your head whirl.

In Joan Hohl's successful trilogy for Silhouette Desire—*Texas Gold* (7/86), *California Copper* (10/86), *Nevada Silver* (1/87)—Joan created a cast of characters that just wouldn't quit. You figure out how *Lady Ice* (5/87) connects. And in August, "J.B." demanded his own story—*One Tough Hombre*. In *Falcon's Flight*, coming in November, you'll learn *all* about . . .?

Annette Broadrick's *Return to Yesterday* (6/87) introduced Adam St. Clair. This August *Adam's Story* tells about the woman who saves his life—and teaches him a thing or two about love!

The six Branigan brothers appeared in Leslie Davis Guccione's *Bittersweet Harvest* (10/86) and *Still Waters* (5/87). September brings *Something in Common*, where the eldest of the strapping Irishmen finds love in unexpected places.

*Midnight Rambler* by Linda Barlow is in October—a special Halloween surprise, and totally unconnected to anything.

Keep an eye out for other Silhouette Desire favorites—Diana Palmer, Dixie Browning, Ann Major and Elizabeth Lowell, to name a few. You never know when secondary characters will insist on their own story. . . .

All the best,

Isabel Swift
Senior Editor & Editorial Coordinator
Silhouette Books

# ANNA SCHMIDT
## Give and Take

Silhouette Desire

Published by Silhouette Books New York

**America's Publisher of Contemporary Romance**

SILHOUETTE BOOKS
300 East 42nd St., New York, N.Y. 10017

Copyright © 1987 by Anna Schmidt

ISBN: 0-373-05381-9

First Silhouette Books printing October 1987

Printed in the U.S.A.

## *ANNA SCHMIDT*

Like her heroine, Marlo, author Anna Schmidt started her career in theatrical design and ended up in visual merchandising. As a free-lance display artist, she ran her own business of creating displays for several high-fashion stores. After the high pressure of the world of retailing, Anna is thoroughly enjoying the relative solitude and freedom that comes with writing.

Anna has lived in New York, Virginia, Chicago, and now makes her home in Wisconsin. Like Marlo, she was hardly prepared for the harsh winters in the beginning but says the cold is like anything else—you get used to it. You don't like it, but you get used to it.

To Anne Leiner,
who showed me that
"Yes, Virginia, there *is* a Santa Claus."

# One

The Christmas tree at Rockefeller Center looked a little smaller that year. A little duller, perhaps. A little more plastic. All of New York seemed a bit plastic to Marlo Fletcher as she strode down Fifth Avenue toward Washington Square.

Marlo was a walker. Let others battle for the cabs, subways and buses. When rush hour struck, Marlo just donned her trusty Nikes and took off. She often walked from Central Park to the Village, where she lived. On today's walk there was none of the storybook charm of Christmas in New York. The city was filthy, thanks to another garbage strike and the bone-chilling wind that blew soot and grime in her face.

She'd been on an appointment to show another producer her set designs in hopes that she'd be chosen to design his new play. The man had been in his early twenties—the latest in a long line of boy wonders to hit the New York theater scene. In the past several seasons, Broadway had followed Hollywood's lead, hoping that youthful directors and producers could revive a drowning business. Marlo had been unimpressed by this particular fair-haired boy. For one thing, she felt positively ancient next to him. She considered herself very liberal and adaptable, able to work with all types of personalities. But this one was beyond her patience. He'd been two hours late for their appointment and had left the room half a dozen times to see friends and take personal calls.

By the time she hit Washington Square, Marlo was fairly stomping her feet into the ground, and as she raced up the front steps of the old building where she lived, her fists were clenched as well as her teeth. "It's your own fault, you know," she admonished the tense reflection that stared back at her from the foyer's cracked mirror as she let herself in through the security door. "If you didn't love your work so much and want to help everybody get shows mounted regardless of whether they can pay you, you might've earned a bit of respect, lady."

Outside her own efficiency apartment she could hear the phone ringing. A ringing phone in New York might mean a job, and at this point she'd even revise her opinion of the boy wonder if he was calling to accept her designs.

Four rings. Five. Why didn't her machine pick up the call? She fumbled with the triple locks on her door until she was able to fling it open and race for the phone. The place was freezing. The super was probably drunk again and had forgotten to turn up the heat. Six rings. Seven.

"Hello? Hello?" Dial tone. She replaced the receiver with an unladylike oath. And then the apartment was silent.

Except for that flapping sound.

Marlo followed the sound to the minute bathroom and saw the blind tapping out a cadence against the open window that led to the fire escape. All over the floor was broken glass.

"Oh, no!" she moaned, and ran back to the large room that served as living and sleeping quarters. "Not again!" she roared to the empty room. She'd been robbed once before. Thus the intricate locks on her door. But this burglar had simply climbed the fire escape and broken the small bathroom window. "The guy was either five years old or anorexic to have gotten through that window," Marlo muttered as she tried to assess the damage. Portable television gone. Cassette recorder. Walkman. Answering machine. He must have had some help. There was no jewelry to speak of—they'd gotten that the last time. The phone started to ring again.

"What?" Marlo barked into the receiver.

"Marlo? It's Patrick Dean. Bloomingdale's. Marlo, are you okay?"

"Patrick!" The memory of handsome blond good looks instantly filled Marlo's thoughts, erasing for the moment the anger and frustration of life in the big city. "Patrick, you're back. I thought we'd lost you to the wilds of Wisconsin."

"Just a visit, Marlo. What the hell's going on over there? You practically shouted my ear off."

"Sorry about that. I've just come from one of the worst days of my short and constantly growing shorter career to find that someone has helped himself—or herself, as the case may be—to my personal belongings for the second time."

"I'm really sorry. Is there anything I can do?"

Spoken like a true New Yorker who knew a simple robbery was hardly worth discussing. It was rapidly becoming a fact of life for people who lived in the city.

"Nope, I'll call the police and file the report, call the insurance guy, pay the higher premiums, and murder the owners of the building if I can find them. After that, how about meeting me for a drink?" She smiled now, relaxing into the easy banter of their old friendship.

"I'll go one better. How about dinner? I'm buying."

"Then you're on an expense account, because as long as I've known you, Patrick Dean, you've never once picked up a check."

He laughed. "Right on all counts. I *am* on an expense account. Not only that, but this is a legitimate business dinner. I have a proposition for you. Interested?"

"Maybe. I thought you were in retailing, though. Have you branched out into theater?"

"The deal is retailing."

"Patrick, that's not my line, and besides, you aren't with Bloomie's anymore, are you?"

"This has nothing to do with Bloomingdale's. Now, will you come out to dinner or not?"

"I'd be crazy not to. My budget hasn't exactly allowed for restaurant eating lately, unless you count pizza by the slice or take-out burgers."

"Great. I'll meet you at the Italian place on Bleecker in forty-five minutes. Wear a red carnation so I'll recognize you." It was an old joke. They'd known each other for years, and with his six-four frame marching next to her five-foot one, they were noticeable in any crowd.

"Give me an hour," Marlo replied. "I have to report my TV, remember?"

When she arrived, Marlo was glad to see that nothing about her friend had changed. He was already at the bar and coming on strong to a leggy blond beauty. Years ago, when they'd first met, Marlo had thought for the briefest instant that there might be a romance between them. But once she'd seen Patrick in action, she'd realized that there could be only heartache in a casual relationship with such a man. She wanted someone willing to commit himself to her, and Patrick was an incurable flirt. She'd long since decided that Patrick's friendship was preferable to his courtship. In friendship he was committed and loyal. In courtship he was unpredictable—a charming trait if one understood the ground rules. The blonde looked as if she might.

"Patrick," Marlo called as she worked her way through the happy-hour crowd to the bar.

"Marlo." Immediately he was off the bar stool and hugging her to his side with one arm. "Meet Sheila." He gestured toward the blonde on the next bar stool who looked as if she might be sizing Marlo up as possible competition.

"Hi." Marlo offered her hand. "Don't worry—we're strictly friends," she said, indicating herself and Patrick, and saw the softening of Sheila's features as she returned Marlo's handshake.

"Nice to meet you, Marlo." The accent was a broad Southern one.

"Look, Sheila," Patrick said, "Marlo and I have some business we need to discuss over dinner. Will you be free later this evening? Can I meet you somewhere?"

"Sure." The young woman had a dazzling smile. "How about here?"

"Okay. Ten o'clock?"

"Great." She gathered her purse and coat and headed for the door. "I'll just go freshen up, long day pounding the pavement, you know. Bye."

"Bye." Patrick imitated her accent and waved.

Marlo giggled. "You're really something. You can't be left alone in this city for half a day before you find the most beautiful woman around and make a date."

"Nice to know I haven't lost my touch, except with you, of course. But then, I'm not your type, am I?"

"Nope. I don't know what it is, but men who are tall and golden-haired with the smile and intelligence of Robert Redford just don't do a thing for me."

"How do you feel about dark and maybe six feet, with blue eyes and a brain like a computer? He doesn't smile much, but then, he's never met you."

"Patrick, what are you babbling about?"

"Oh, no. That's getting ahead of the story. First we talk about work. What are you doing these days?"

"Not a lot, I'm afraid. The past season has been dismal, and the one ahead looks even worse. I may actually have to take a *real job*."

"Oh, no, not that," Patrick cried in mock horror. "Have you ever considered doing windows?"

"Excuse me?"

"Windows. Displays for stores. Visual merchandising."

"Oh." Marlo had often admired the store windows during her walks through the city. There was something very theatrical about the better ones. "No, I guess not," she answered.

"Well, start thinking about it, because I need you to help me out of a major jam."

"Wait a minute. Are we talking major jam in New York, or back there on the prairie?"

"Milwaukee is a metropolitan area, and Wisconsin is not exactly the prairie. Close, but not exactly."

"You're dreaming, my friend. New York may have me down for the moment, but I can't leave. This is where I'm from. I don't know anywhere else. I wouldn't know how to be anywhere else."

"It's sad that you think that." Patrick's expression grew serious. "For a freewheeling New Yorker, you certainly have limited horizons."

"You know what I mean. I'm a designer. My work needs an audience."

"What do you think window artists work for? They're designers. They need audiences."

"But Milwaukee," she lamented, as if it were the end of the world.

"Forget that it's Milwaukee for the moment. Let's talk about something near and dear to your heart and stomach. Money."

"I'm listening." She had to. Her checkbook read next to nothing, and there were only a couple of dips left in her savings.

Patrick named a figure and listed benefits that sounded like a fortune to Marlo, who'd grown accustomed to the uncertainty of a life lived from one job to the next.

"What do I have to do for that, promise my firstborn?"

"Nothing like that. Here's the story. The store I work for is called Carrington's. Several decades ago it was *the* store north of Chicago. Then the business fell on hard times. Now my friend, Josh Carrington, is trying to bring it back up to the status it held when his grandfather founded the place. By investing huge chunks of his own money, over the last few years Josh has put together a top staff, including George Garber, our display and merchandising designer. Last week George had a major heart attack. The reports on his recovery spell several months of recuperation, and we're just on the brink of the spring fashion season. Without top merchandising, we'll lose ground. Here's the dilemma: how to keep on paying George during his convalescence *and* hire someone capable of handling the job. We want George back, and that means we can't offer his job to anyone who's looking for something permanent, so..."

Marlo was fascinated. She'd never known Patrick to be so serious about anything, and the story of the store's comeback sounded like the makings of a hit Broadway show. "Wow, you're really into this."

Patrick leaned back and sipped his drink. "I guess I am. Josh is an old friend, but he's really more like a brother. We met at Harvard—roomed together. We're both only children of wealthy parents who spent a lot of time traveling and leaving us with surrogates. We each had big plans for making it in the retailing world. I came to the Big Apple, and he went home to Milwaukee."

"And how did you come to be there, in Milwaukee?" Marlo was intrigued by this man Josh, who had so much influence that Patrick would have given up the bright lights of New York for the Midwest.

"Josh called one day. His father had just been killed—he raced cars in Europe half the time when he should've been minding the store—and suddenly Josh was in charge of the family business. He was determined to prove himself. He'd been working in the store since college, and some of the taint that was on his father had clung to him. Now, when we're so close to success, George... Let's just say we can't finish the job without top-notch merchandising."

"But I'm a *theatrical* designer. I know zilch about retailing."

"The retail business is pure and simple show biz, Marlo. You're perfect. Say you'll help."

"For how long?" She couldn't believe she was actually considering the idea.

"Just until George is back on his feet—six months tops, maybe less. Just get us through the spring opening." He was leaning across the table, clutching her hands between his. "Will you please come? For me? For Josh?"

"For Josh? I don't even know the man."

Patrick grinned and relaxed. He studied her for a long moment. "Ah, but you will. And you, my friend, are going to turn that man's life inside out. Believe me, you're exactly what he needs. I can't wait."

"Hold it, Patrick. What are you plotting?" Marlo had played roles in some of her friend's elaborate schemes before. The man was a born matchmaker when it came to people he liked, and Marlo knew that he liked her and obviously this Josh a lot. "I'm in the market for a paying job, not a love life."

"What can it hurt? If it happens, it happens. Let me tell you about him—at least the basics."

"I'll make my own observations, okay? Now, when do you plan on my being there?"

"How about yesterday? Too soon? Okay, I'm flying back the day after tomorrow. I'd love for you to come with me so I can fill you in over the weekend and you can get started Monday. We haven't had a new display on the avenue since George got sick."

"Patrick, I can't be ready to go in two days. What about my apartment? I have to find somebody to sublet. I have to pack. My agent has a couple of interviews lined up for me. Three weeks—that's the absolute earliest I can leave." Her mind was already whirling with lists and details to be arranged.

"The day after New Year's, and that's the limit. I'll go back to Milwaukee and find you a place to live, okay? Do we have a deal?"

"I'm crazy enough to do this. But you already knew that before you flew out here, didn't you?"

"Yep. Yesterday I was sitting in my office in Milwaukee, pondering the spring opening, and I thought about the set you did for those two fashion designers down in Soho, remember?" Marlo nodded. "Well, in that moment I knew exactly who could bail us out of this jam. Marlo Fletcher, the best undiscovered designer on or off Broadway." He raised his glass in a toast.

Marlo lifted hers in an answer that sealed their bargain. "Are you really authorized to pay me that much money every month?"

"Not exactly. But Josh will buy it once he gets a look at you and what you're going to do for his store."

"Patrick, I'm having second thoughts—"

"Nope, not allowed. A deal's a deal. Now, let's order. I'm famished, and Sheila awaits."

* * *

The holidays passed in a blur. Marlo spent Christmas on Long Island with the rest of her family. The holiday season was one long party at the Fletcher home, and she hated cutting short their time together. Her brothers and sisters and parents were eager to hear what on earth could entice their Marlo to leave New York for Milwaukee.

Her sister Vicki, an actress who'd played in some road companies, warned her to pack only her warmest clothing. "And even that won't be enough," she said with a frown. Her mother, ever the romantic, was far more intrigued with Marlo's stories of Josh Carrington. "Just remember to keep an open mind, dear. The man sounds fascinating, regardless of where he lives."

That night Marlo hurried back to the city to make a dent in her packing. After their dinner, Patrick had called to say that Sheila was looking for an apartment to sublet until she got her bearings. Marlo checked her out over the next week, having lunch with Sheila twice before deciding the newcomer could be trusted to take care of her things and keep the apartment locked and reasonably secured against burglars. "After all, what's left to attract them?" she asked Sheila with a shrug.

"My stuff," Sheila grumbled, and they both laughed.

By New Year's Eve Marlo was packed and had her plane tickets, which Patrick had sent the week before. He certainly was pulling out all the stops, she marveled. She spent the evening at a favorite Village hangout with as many of her friends and family members as she could gather and suffered their good-humored jabs at the idea that she was leaving New York and the theater for a job in a department store in Milwaukee, of all places.

The following afternoon she was on her way. As the plane circled the Milwaukee airport, her first impression was of snow. There seemed to be no end to it. Marlo was glad she'd decided to wear her boots on the plane. Now she just hoped the pilot could find a place to land. She had her doubts, since his choice seemed to be limited to snow or water.

"Welcome to Wisconsin—nature's wonderland," Patrick sang out as he twirled her around when the plane had landed and she'd entered the airport.

"Is it as cold as it looks out there?" Marlo was definitely having second thoughts. In contrast to the bustle and chaos of La Guardia, the Milwaukee airport seemed like the inside of a church. On top of that, while New York had its share of nasty weather, there was something about this particular snowy landscape that looked permanent.

"Trust me. By the time you've spent a couple of weeks here, you'll be a regular snow bunny."

"Right," Marlo replied doubtfully.

They collected her luggage and loaded it into the back of Patrick's vintage sports car. Marlo's teeth were chattering. "Does this thing have a heater?" she asked as they headed into the city.

"Comes and goes," was Patrick's succinct explanation.

"Any chance it might come in the next hour?"

"We'll be at your place well before then. Well, what do you think?" He gestured grandly toward the skyline, such as it was.

The thing that caught Marlo's attention was not the buildings' lack of height. It was the incredible clarity of the view. She could actually see stars, and the city fairly gleamed beneath the full moon as they approached. She rolled down the window and hung her head out to breathe in the crystal-clear night air.

"I thought you were cold," Patrick shouted above the noise of the car and the expressway.

"You didn't tell me about the fresh air. I mean, Patrick, air that you can see through, that you can breathe in without wheezing it back out, that doesn't leave a layer of grime on you.... This is incredible!"

"I offer the woman top dollar plus perks and all she wants is a little fresh air. Will you roll up the window, for heaven's sake?"

"Done. Where are we headed now?" He'd taken an exit off the expressway and was driving toward the lights of downtown.

"I thought I'd give you the nickel tour—a drive up the avenue past Carrington's, then along the magnificent lake, and then home."

"Let's start with home. What did you find for me?"

"You'll be living with Josh."

"So finally you admit there's more than working in the store attached to earning this salary. Patrick, I don't sleep with my bosses, no matter what you may have heard about the world of theater."

"Not even if you fall for them and they fall for you, which in this case is guaranteed to happen?"

"Patrick, be serious. What about my living arrangements?"

"Okay. There's this carriage house on the Carrington estate, and the second floor is the most charming little apartment. It even has a fireplace—very cozy."

"Are there a closet, a bed and a kitchen?"

"Absolutely. You'll be impressed. Trust me."

"The more you keep saying that, the more concerned I become. Couldn't you just have found me something in a high rise near the store? I don't have a car, you know."

"But you adore walking, and the store is within walking distance for you—three, four miles tops. Besides, in a very short time you'll be riding back and forth with the boss man himself. Trust me."

Marlo groaned. "Is this Josh actually condoning your mail-order matchmaking?"

"He doesn't know a thing about it—or you, for that matter. The man is so into worrying about raising the money to bail his store out of the red that he's barely aware that George is in the hospital."

"Sounds pretty insensitive," Marlo said huffily. She had to admit that until that moment she'd been somewhat intrigued by the mysterious head of the department store.

"Josh is the champion softie. It's just that his secretary and I decided to play down the crisis in merchandising, hoping to prevent a stroke."

"How old is Josh?"

"Same as me, thirty-four. We went to college together, remember?"

"I know, but you mentioned a stroke. I suddenly envisioned an old man in a wheelchair."

"Ah, that would be Joshua Carrington the first, Josh's grandfather and the founder of the business you've arrived in the nick of time to rescue. J.P. is in his late seventies, and in a wheelchair, following a losing battle with arthritis. However, don't be fooled. The man is a patriarch in the truest sense of the word. He rules that family, especially Josh."

Marlo noticed a slightly bitter tone in Patrick's voice.

"And how did I wind up in the carriage house if no one knows I'm coming?"

"Sally Carrington knows. She's Josh's mother and the source of any charm and sweetness currently residing in that gloomy old mausoleum. She's my ally, and she'll be yours, too. The woman's beside herself with curiosity to meet you, but I've persuaded her to hold off until tomorrow.... Well, here's the store. What do you think?"

While they'd talked, Patrick had maneuvered the car down what he identified as the main street, Wisconsin Avenue. On one side of the street she noted the enclosed mall that ran for several blocks, housing stores and restaurants, anchored at either end by what appeared to be two major department stores. There were also skywalks connecting it to other buildings, one walk spanning a river. She noticed that once they'd crossed the river, the stores were smaller and interspersed between large office complexes and bank buildings. Patrick had identified this section as East Town, and he'd pointed out with a grin that one side of their store faced onto a street called Broadway.

He parked in front of a square four-story building that reeked of class and history and tradition. Marlo was impressed in spite of herself. The lighted windows that lined the avenue were dramatically designed and eye-catching. This George certainly knew his stuff.

"When do I get to meet George?" she asked as Patrick led her past the night watchman and into the dimly lit store. "I think he's going to be able to teach me a lot." Her mind was already clicking with new ideas as they walked up and down the aisles of the elegant store. Patrick kept up a running commentary on what they'd tried to achieve since Josh had taken over as president of the business. He knew Marlo was registering every word and that she'd only have to be told once. Her on-the-job training had begun the minute they'd left the car.

By the time they'd returned to his car and continued their tour along the avenue, Marlo was bombarding Patrick with questions. In between answers, Patrick tried to point out the local landmarks—the art center, the yacht club, the beaches. The lake itself was like black satin, stretching as far as the eye could see. Marlo was completely captivated by the proximity of such contrasts—a viable commercial area and then, two minutes away, this huge lake with beaches and parks and boat slips.

"It's really lovely, isn't it?"

"Yeah, it is." There was no mistaking the trace of pride in Patrick's voice. "It's not New York, but I think you'll be pleasantly surprised at what it has to offer—especially the sophistication of the people."

They'd left the lake behind and took a shortcut through a park. "Wahl Avenue, my dear. Some of the richest men in the Midwest started their families in these homes, including J. P. Carrington."

"The first?"

"The first. He married money—a beer baron's daughter. But he also made his own. Well, here we are. Home, sweet home."

"Oh, my!" Marlo couldn't manage much more than that as they pulled up to a large stone house that faced the lake. To one side was what Marlo could only describe as the most elegant garage she'd ever seen. The main house was lit as if every room was in use.

"It's very—" Marlo stumbled to find a word "—bright."

Patrick chuckled as they stopped next to the double garage doors. "Sally keeps the place lit up like a Christmas tree most of the time—drives the old man crazy."

Marlo followed Patrick up a stairway at one side of the carriage house. She took in the solidity of the building—stone supported by wide plank beams. The large heavy wood door swung in to reveal a small foyer and the lady of the house herself.

"Sally." Patrick didn't seem surprised to see the present Mrs. Carrington waiting for them in the small apartment. "I thought we agreed you'd wait until morning to meet your new tenant." His words were reproving, but his smile and tone were filled with teasing. "Sally Carrington, Marlo Fletcher."

The two women shook hands, and then Sally was off leading the grand tour as if she were showing off Buckingham Pal-
ace. She talked nonstop, making conversation unnecessary for
either Patrick or Marlo. Marlo was grateful, because it gave her
a chance to get her bearings.

Marlo wondered if the main house could possibly be any
more elegant than this one. There were cathedral ceilings with
heavy wood beams, and the polished wood floors were covered with worn Oriental rugs. The furnishings were old country French, and the promised fireplace was even laid and ready
to be lit. "Living room, dining area," Sally said, indicating
them with a wave of her well-manicured hand as she headed
down a short hallway, turning on lights as she went. "Kitchen
here, bedroom there, bath. All the comforts of home. Let me
run through some of the basics for you—heat controls, keys,
that sort of thing."

Marlo didn't miss the care that had been taken in getting this
place ready to receive her. The phone was installed. The bed
was made. There were fresh flowers in every room. The refrigerator and cupboards were filled. There were even towels in the
bathroom. She didn't need a thing except her clothes.

"Mrs. Carrington, I'm overwhelmed. You certainly know
how to make a person feel welcome," Marlo observed when the
three of them had returned to the living room, where a steaming pot of tea waited.

"It's Sally, dear, and I had a ball getting this place together
for you. It has a real homey feeling, don't you think?"

"I think it probably reflects its owners. I can't wait to meet
the rest of the family." She glanced at Patrick, her eyes twin-
kling, but his were serious.

"Marlo, about Josh. Sally and I were thinking it would be
better if you got your feet wet first. Fortunately, he has to be
out of town for the next couple of days. This way you'll have
time to get in there and execute a couple of designs. I'll give you
all the support and manpower you need."

"How much manpower did George use?"

"George worked alone, but—"

"Then I will, too. In fact, I prefer it, especially in the beginning. Just give me someone for a few days who knows where

everything is in the store and around town, and I'll take it from there." They drank their tea in silence. "You haven't given Josh any idea about my coming, have you, Patrick?"

He had the decency to look abashed for a moment, and she noticed that Sally smothered a smile as she placed her teacup on the wooden tray.

"Josh is running pretty much on raw nerve these days," Patrick replied. "His fuse tends to be pretty short, and at the moment he's not too receptive to new concepts. His mind is focused on taking the store back to its former grandeur. Sometimes that gets in the way of his being able to see the future clearly. But you can help him and the business, Marlo. I know you can. You're exactly the person we need right now, and before you know it, Josh will know that, too. I really appreciate your coming."

"Sounds like more than your friendship with Josh is at stake here."

He shrugged. "I admit I have higher ambitions than Milwaukee. If I can have a part in pulling this off, perhaps I can write my own ticket. With my experience in New York and now this, it might be possible to go wherever I want—Beverly Hills, Dallas—"

"I'm noticing a trend toward warmth and sunshine," Sally teased.

"Well, now that Marlo's really here and I can see she's already hooked on the challenge, I'll admit it. The winters in this place can be a bear." He grinned and shivered.

"Gee, and someone just told me in a couple of weeks I'd be a regular snow bunny," Marlo reminded him.

"Oh, you will—" Patrick smiled "—you will. Just let Josh work his magic on you and you'll never want to leave. Trust me."

"Stop saying that," Marlo moaned, and Sally laughed as the three of them walked together to the front door.

"Good night, Marlo, and welcome to our home. I think you are going to be just what my son needs. Thank you for coming." Sally Carrington hugged Marlo warmly, as did Patrick, and then they were gone.

Marlo found she was too keyed-up to consider sleeping for several hours yet. She called her parents to tell them of her safe arrival and first impressions. She unpacked as she planned designs for windows in her head. She could hardly wait to tackle the showcases that lined the avenue and side streets. She phoned Patrick and told him she wanted him at the apartment first thing in the morning to take her to the hospital to meet George Garber.

She fixed herself a bowl of cereal and wandered around the apartment as she ate. She peered out each of the small-paned windows and noticed that the main house was now dark, except for one golden light in an upstairs window. After she had washed out her bowl and spoon, she looked around for a place to store her luggage. The place might be long on charm, but it was pretty short on storage space. Marlo had noticed a closet in the foyer, and looking in there now, she found it empty, with the exception of a couple of open cardboard boxes. She decided she could move them around until her luggage would fit.

The cartons were heavy. Inside were several books and framed photographs. On closer inspection, Marlo realized that the books were family photo albums. Curious, she dragged the cartons to the sofa, wrapped herself in the down comforter that'd been tossed over one arm of the couch and settled in to meet the Carrington family. Perhaps Patrick wanted to hold off introducing her to Josh Carrington, but he hadn't said anything about her getting a head start by looking through the albums.

Two hours later she had a clear picture of Sally Carrington—a woman of beauty, wit and a highly developed sense of personal style. Sally had clowned through several poses over the years covered by the numerous albums. She was always dressed in the latest fashions, accented with her own individual touch—a flowing scarf, a dramatic brooch. Marlo had liked the woman instantly and believed that Patrick had been correct in predicting a fast friendship between the two of them.

Josh's father—Carrington number two—could've played the title role in *Playboy of the Western World* without a hitch. The man looked the very definition of suave and debonair. But behind the flashing teeth was something of the little boy. His position in the photograph was always center stage. Everyone else was in the background, and while others might watch him, his eyes were for the camera alone.

J. P. Carrington was another story. Oh, he radiated sternness and an iron will, but there was something there that Marlo found attractive, likable. She recognized a certain willfulness in the unflinching stare with which the old man met the camera. She was familiar with that particular brand of stubbornness—it stared back at her every morning from her own mirror. This man clearly enjoyed a challenge, and also, if she was any judge of character, he would appreciate daring.

And then there was her new employer—Joshua Carrington III. There were dozens of photographs of the young Master Carrington, even down to the obligatory bare-bottom-on-a-bearskin-rug. And yet even in his later years, the photographs gave little clue as to what he might be like. As he matured, he always seemed to seek out the background in a group pose, and often he'd moved just as the camera snapped, so that he was slightly out of focus.

Marlo had the impression of dark good looks—heavy brows over wide-set eyes that were practically hidden by thick black lashes. His nose was a shade too long and slightly crooked. In the earliest pictures his ears stood out, and she assumed he'd endured a lot of ribbing about that at school. Later he'd learned to style his hair so that they were covered. Marlo smiled. Physically he was a very appealing man, and she figured if she'd seen him in New York, she would've been tempted to meet him.

She would've liked to see his smile. But once he'd passed his tenth birthday, he seemed to have given up on the idea of smiling. He was always very solemn, as if the camera were an enemy, not a pleasure. His mouth was often set in a firm line, and there was little humor in his dark blue eyes. There was determination and intelligence and energy, but no humor.

Marlo put away the albums and framed pictures. But she continued to see the face of Josh Carrington long after she'd prepared herself for bed. Perhaps Patrick was right about her guaranteed attraction to the man. Certainly she couldn't deny that she was intrigued or that she'd been curious from the first she'd heard of him. She loved life and people and the mix of the two. She enjoyed watching people meet their personal challenges, and from what Patrick had told her, Josh Carrington was facing the challenge of his life at this moment. It was exciting for her to be a part of that for someone else. She locked her hands behind her head as she stared out at the cold, clear night. The images of the youthful, adolescent and adult man who was to be her new employer danced in her mind. That face didn't seem to be one easily defeated by any blow life might choose to deal him, she decided.

Patrick knew her too well. In fact, she wouldn't put it past him to have had Sally plant those albums, betting that sooner or later Marlo would discover them. Marlo knew Patrick equally well, and he wasn't above setting up two people to play out a romance he'd invented. One of these days she was going to set up just such a situation for her old friend Patrick Dean and see how much he liked being on the other end.

# Two

———

Josh's mood was as foul as the weather. While others picked their way cautiously through the gray snowbanks lining Wisconsin Avenue, Joshua Carrington III strode determinedly toward the store his grandfather had founded, which had anchored the east end of the avenue for three-quarters of a century. That store had nearly been ruined when Josh's father turned it into a four-story bargain basement during the hard times of the seventies.

Carrington's. The name dominated the view as he walked east across the Milwaukee River. East Town had once been a fashion mecca of exclusive shops and galleries. Many of them had either given up or been forced out in the past decade. Some had moved to more profitable locations in the suburbs, and some had simply closed their doors. Josh Carrington had a dream that East Town would thrive again. There were still enough of the old quality shops to form a base. Watt's, with its fine crystal and china, and the only elegant tearoom in the city; Zita's; Peacock's; the grand old Pfister Hotel; and Carrington's.

It had started to snow, and the wind was howling down the avenue from the lake. Josh turned up his collar and bent into the driving force of the wind as if it were another adversary to be beaten. He was almost across the street when he noticed a small crowd gathered outside a corner window of his store. It was the noon hour, when the surrounding government and office complexes emptied their thousands of employees into the avenue and its side streets. But normally in mid-January the crowds wouldn't give more than a glance to his store as they rushed west to the mall for lunch and indoor shopping. These people were standing in near-zero cold to see something that was happening in the window of his store.

Josh crossed against the light and worked his way into the crowd. The first thing he noticed was a kaleidoscope of color playing off a completely black background. Neon yellows and pinks and greens grabbed even the most casual observer. Against the bitter cold of the gray January day, such hot color was difficult to ignore. Six mannequins—some standing, others lounging against walls—directed the eye to circle the window until every piece of merchandise had been noticed. Suddenly one mannequin came to life.

With a start Josh realized that the petite woman who was dressing the window had by her stance and costume become such a part of the total picture that it was unnerving to see her move. He watched along with the others, absorbed in the magic she was creating for them. Her short dark hair was wrapped in a canary-yellow scarf tied to one side in a perky bow. She wore black leather slacks, and her oversize white shirt was opened to the waist to reveal a bright green tank over a hot pink T-shirt. Her small waist was secured by not one but three belts, which she removed one at a time to drape around the mannequins, and she was shoeless, exposing print socks that picked up the bright colors of her outfit.

Her movements in the confines of the window were sure and graceful, and her face was a study in concentration as she perfected the scene. One strand of mannequin hair out of place was enough to command her attention. After motioning to those outside to wait, she left the window and in seconds had joined them on the street. She'd put on ankle-high boots and wrapped herself in a large woolen shawl. "What do you think?" she asked the observers as she made her way to the center of the group.

Her fans were staunchly loyal: "It's great." "Don't touch it." "You're going to freeze."

"I've got just the thing," she said, and raced back inside the store. A moment later she was back in the window and placing sunglasses on two of the mannequins. The lenses were shaped like stars, and the frames were bright orange. She turned and grinned at her audience, awaiting their approval. As one, the group grinned back and gave her the thumbs-up sign, then scattered to continue their lunch hours in warmer surroundings. Only Josh Carrington stood on the now-empty sidewalk.

For an instant their eyes met. In hers he caught a glimmer of recognition, and then she smiled warmly and nodded. Her smile was infectious, and he felt the beginnings of a smile coming to his own mouth—but he suppressed it. This woman obviously worked for him, and he didn't even know it. He prided himself on knowing each of his employees personally. He set his shoulders and headed for the revolving-door entrance so that he could rectify this particular oversight.

But by the time Josh had walked through the store to the window, the woman had gathered her supplies and left, presumably to get her own lunch. Though her tiny stature suggested that she never ate, her full mouth was beautifully expressive, and her high cheekbones would have been the envy of many a model Josh knew. But that wasn't the point. The point was that somehow this human dynamo had created interest in his store. As they walked away, the people had been discussing the store, its fashion image, merchandise and prices. Josh considered going directly to the display department and promoting this young lady to something akin to chairperson of the board, then decided that that such a move would be completely out of character for him. Josh Carrington rarely acted against his own highly disciplined character.

When he got to his fourth-floor office, the phone was ringing. "It's your mother, dear," the voice on the other end announced unnecessarily. "How did it go with the bank?"

"They still turned me down, Mother."

"Really? How extraordinarily shortsighted of them. Well, never mind. That isn't what I called about. I called to remind you to put next Friday's dinner here with the symphony committee on your calendar."

"Mother..."

"Now, I won't listen to a no, Josh. This is important for you and the store."

"Mother," Josh interrupted her again, "the only thing that's important to the store at this point is having the money to finance the changes we're trying to make. If we're going to pull this off, we have to be able to stock the finest merchandise, and the designers in New York are reluctant to even talk to us unless we have the cash in hand."

"Yes, I know. That's all thanks to your father—such a charming man, but absolutely no head for business. Well, I think you should forget the New York collections. Everyone stocks them anyway. You need to find some new and unusual resources—West Coast punk or whatever they're doing out there these days."

"Mother, I'm due at a meeting." Josh knew that once his mother got started she could be impossible to get off the subject of new ideas for merchandising the store. Not that he didn't appreciate her savvy; it was just that at the moment he had other things on his mind.

"Joshua Carrington, don't you dare hang up on me! Now, you be here for this committee dinner, and do try to bring someone interesting. I don't know how you hope to create any excitement for the business when your own life is so terribly predictable and boring."

"Are you calling my dates boring?" He smiled for the first time since he'd left the bank and felt some of his tension dissolve. His mother had a knack for doing that to people.

"You know very well they are, regardless of the fact they come from the best families and the oldest money—maybe that's what makes them so stuffy. Honestly, dear, I can't tell one from the other, and if the truth be told, I don't think you can either. That's probably why you keep bringing different ones to every function I throw. You're not getting any younger, you know, and I'd really like to enjoy my grandchildren before I'm too old to recognize them."

"Mother, how did we get from a simple dinner party to bouncing grandchildren on your knee?"

"We all have to start somewhere, and dinner is as good a place as any. So, Friday, eight o'clock. I know! Why don't you bring Marlo?"

"Marlo?"

"Marlo Fletcher, dear. She works for you. She lives in the carriage house. Josh?"

"Mother, I don't have any idea what you are talking about."

There was the slightest pause before Sally answered. "Have you spoken to Patrick lately, dear? He assured me he would handle that end." The last comment was made almost to herself.

"I sent Patrick to New York. He just got back, and we haven't had the time to talk. What would Patrick have to do with someone living in our carriage house, Mother?"

"Er, I think someone is at the door. Talk to Patrick, dear. Goodbye." And she was gone. Josh knew there hadn't been anyone at the door. Sally Carrington had been caught in one of her frequent matchmaking schemes and had hung up before he could question her further.

Josh cradled the phone on one shoulder and buzzed his secretary, as he riffled through the stacks of outgoing mail on his desk. "Wilma, ask Mr. Dean to stop in here as soon as possible, please." Josh replaced the receiver and swiveled to confront the calendar that dominated one wall of his office. It was his blueprint for the revitalization of Carrington's, and up until a few weeks before, they'd been right on schedule. Then George Garber had had his heart attack. Josh sighed heavily. At this point they'd have to work a great deal of overtime to meet the deadline he'd set for himself—unless he could find a small miracle.

His mind returned to how the woman in the window had captivated everyone watching her—including himself. He found himself replaying the details of her appearance, her manner. The way she would suddenly sweep her long fingers through her short, shaggy hair when she was thinking. The grace with which she manipulated the heavy mannequins as if they were weightless until she'd achieved just the right position. The laughter in her large dark eyes as she added just that touch of humor the window needed in order to say, "These are clothes not to be taken too seriously. These are clothes for letting go in—for having fun in." The sunglasses had been the perfect touch.

"You buzzed, O great leader?" Patrick smiled as he took the chair opposite Josh and settled his large frame into it. Patrick Dean had been Josh's best friend for nearly twenty years, and when Josh had called him to help save Carrington's, he'd left a lucrative position with Bloomingdale's in New York, risking a bright future in retailing there to come to Milwaukee. Neither of them regretted that decision.

"Who is Marlo Fletcher, and why is she living in our carriage house?" Josh had a reputation for coming directly to the point.

"Aha. You have either (a) spoken to your mother, (b) noticed the new look in the store, or (c) all of the above." Patrick grinned at him. "I wondered when you'd notice something. I thought by now you'd at least have noticed the lights in the carriage house."

"I've been a little preoccupied. She's George's replacement? Did you steal her from Field's or Boston Store?" Josh knew that Patrick liked to raid the competition periodically for talented staff to fill key positions at Carrington's. Josh wasn't particularly fond of the habit, but he had to admit that it produced results.

"She's from Broadway." Clearly Patrick was enjoying himself.

"Broadway? You mean Hunter's?" Josh was referring to an exclusive store on the side street that had decided to close its doors.

"Broadway as in bright lights, the Great White Way, New York."

Josh sat down in the high-backed chair across from his friend. "I think I want to hear this from the beginning," he said, suspicious.

"Last month, after George got sick, I was at a loss. There's just no one in the Midwest who can hold a candle to George—

at least no one who would be willing to fill in temporarily. Anyway, I was watching a play at the Rep when it hit me. Marlo Fletcher. She's a New York stage designer. She does mostly off-Broadway and guest spots for regional theater, but she's damned creative.''

''And how were you able to entice this blossoming star to chuck it all for the subzero winter of Milwaukee?''

Again, Patrick flashed him the grin that had charmed the socks off people from eight to eighty. ''I told her it was only temporary. I also played on our friendship and gambled on the fact that for as long as I've known her, the woman has been incapable of turning down a chance to design, especially if the job involves pressure. I've never met anyone who thrives on pressure the way Marlo does.''

''There's a punch line, right?''

''Actually, there is. It looks like George might be moving on to something less stressful—like an early retirement.''

''Damn.'' Josh brought his fist down forcefully on his desk. ''We've worked too hard all these months building a team that can carry us through on this.'' He indicated the calendar behind him with the spring opening circled in red. ''Display and promotion are the keys to pulling this off, Patrick.''

''You don't like what Marlo's doing?'' Patrick looked confused.

''I do. At least what I saw this morning. That corner window is dynamite. She had an audience, for crying out loud. But in those positions we need people who understand retailing, Patrick, not Broadway designers.''

''Marlo's a quick study. Believe me. She can learn this business, and in the meantime she can bring us a look no one else can begin to duplicate. People from all over will be copying us, Josh. Isn't that what this is all about?''

''Okay, let's say for argument's sake that she works out. You told her it was temporary. We get her trained, educated to the business, and she gets an offer to do a show and takes off. We have to have some stability, Pat. It's the backbone of what we're trying to build.''

"I told her it was temporary to get her to come. I think that between you, Sally and me we can seduce Marlo into staying right here as a permanent member of the Carrington team."

"What's Mother got to do with this?"

"We were having lunch one day after I came back from New York and I was telling her about Marlo. The more I told her, the brighter her smile became. She's the one who suggested the carriage house when I told her Marlo would need a furnished place to stay."

"I detect some matchmaking going on here. Pat, my mother is an incurable romantic who's been trying to marry me off for the past ten years. I hope I wasn't part of the deal you offered Ms. Fletcher." He studied his vice president through narrowed eyes, alert to the slightest clue that this whole deal was a setup to get him romantically involved.

"Come on, Josh, Marlo's very independent. The minute I mentioned the idea that she might even *like* her new boss, she bristled and showed her claws. I backed off right away. You two would be perfect for each other, but neither of you has the good sense to recognize that. You'll both be too busy trying to do your jobs." He saw that Josh believed him and relaxed.

"You really think she can grasp what we want?" Josh was frowning.

"The woman is fabulous. Get your nose out of those balance sheets and watch her work. She's doing the southeast corner window this afternoon. Want to meet her?"

"Of course I want to meet her. She may have just been handed the third most important job in this organization. I should've met her weeks ago—*before* she was hired. But I'll handle it in my own way, Patrick. No prior warnings, understood?"

"Fine. Just be prepared, scout. Marlo Fletcher has been known to knock more than one man off his feet, and you, my friend, have been ripe for a long time."

"Did she do that to you?" Suddenly Josh was abnormally interested in the exact nature of the relationship between his best friend and the dark beauty who was designing his windows.

"Not to worry. We've been friends from the beginning—her choice and mine. There's something about Marlo that calls for permanence and commitment, and we both know that's not my style. Now you, on the other hand—"

"This is business, Pat," Josh growled, and pulled the ledgers across the desk as he willed himself to erase the sudden image of dark laughing eyes above a full mouth that invited further exploration.

"Okay, but don't say you weren't warned. Catch you later," Patrick said, strolling out the door, then closing it behind him.

The afternoon was filled with calls and meetings, and it was after four before Josh got the chance to check out the display being installed in the southeast window. When he arrived, Marlo was nowhere to be seen, so he took the opportunity to look around and observe her work in progress. The large window had been converted into an intimate Victorian boudoir. With Valentine's Day just a month away, Marlo had selected a theme of romantic lingerie. The four-poster dummy bed was dressed in lace-trimmed linens and a satin comforter. A filmy negligee was tossed across the foot of the bed in a most inviting way.

"Hello?"

Josh turned toward the soft voice, surprised at how deep it was, belonging as it did to such a small woman. He suddenly felt embarrassed, as if he'd caught a lady in a most private moment. Marlo Fletcher paused at the entrance to the window. She was carrying a silver tea service set for two. She was still wearing the leather slacks and overshirt, but now the shirt was buttoned to the throat and a tiny wisp of lace peeked from the breast pocket. Her large liquid eyes were wide with questions.

"Hello. Joshua Carrington." He offered his hand but quickly withdrew it when he saw she could hardly shake hands and balance the tea tray at the same time. "Patrick told me where to find you. Here, let me help with that." Josh reached for the tray and set it on the marble-topped round table in one corner. He was surprised to see steam rising from the spout of the ornate teapot, and there was fresh lemon in the side dish.

"Of course," she said, offering her hand once he'd turned back to her. "I'm happy to meet you at last. Since he called me in New York, Patrick's been raving about your efforts to practically revolutionize your business. You're not at all what I expected." Marlo had gone back to her work, but scrutinized him over one shoulder as she knelt next to the bed and re-draped the negligee.

Josh wasn't sure he liked the way things were going. She was, after all, an employee, and her frank gaze made him feel uncomfortable. On top of that, he had no idea what Patrick and his mother might have already told her. He felt as if he were being interviewed and needed to measure up to her standards. Not that her look was unfriendly. There seemed always to be a hint of a smile or even laughter just beyond her calm exterior. "What did you expect?" he asked a bit stiffly.

"I think someone a little harder around the edges." She smiled, then grew serious. "Although you are very... mature, aren't you?"

"Meaning?" From Josh's tone, it was obvious to her that her words had come out wrong.

"Uh-oh. I'm getting off on the wrong foot, aren't I?" Marlo rose and crossed in front of him. The window wasn't that large, and she had to pass very close to get to the other side of the bed. She had the creamiest skin he'd ever seen, and there wasn't a speck of makeup covering it. "How about a truce and some tea?" she asked, lifting one fragile cup.

Josh nodded, then perched on the edge of a delicate rosewood chair. He watched as she served him, and he became aware that the tea was not the only touch of reality she'd brought to the window—strains of a Mozart concerto came from a small FM radio. And the air was filled with some musky, moody perfume, perfect in this atmosphere of pink lighting and romantic afternoons. Marlo was wearing the perfume. He might have been in her bedroom sharing tea with her before an afternoon of lovemaking. Suddenly Josh realized that the street traffic had disappeared, and he ran one finger under his collar to relieve the flush he felt rising there.

"Now, shall we begin again? I'm Marlo Fletcher, and I'm not sure what Patrick or your mother might have told you. I'm very sorry not to have stopped by earlier to introduce myself, but when I arrived, you were out of town. The few times I tried since then you were either out or in a meeting. How's your tea?''

She'd settled cross-legged on the Oriental rug at his feet and was looking up at him with wide, animated eyes. He noticed that she talked with her hands as well as with her incredibly expressive face. It wasn't that she was beautiful in the classic sense. What she was, Josh decided, was sexy. He felt as if he wanted to do more than get to know her. He wanted to taste her as if she were a luscious dessert. She was smiling up at him now, and he knew it was his turn to say something.

"The tea is fine. Do you always go to so much trouble when you dress a window?"

She shrugged and looked around as she took another sip. "I like to set a mood when I have the time. I've found it helps me to get the message across better if I feel a part of it all. I wanted the impression of a real person living in this room—someone who's just stepped out for a moment and any minute will come through that door."

"So the music, the perfume, the tea—do you change your costume for every display?"

She laughed again. He liked her laugh—it was so open and direct. "I'd be changing all day. No, I start with something basic, like black or beige, and then add or subtract as the mood hits me. It helps me to feel that I belong in the scene, and it also makes me less conspicuous to those who walk by while I'm working." She indicated the street outside the large pane of plate glass that filled one wall of their room. Josh had forgotten for a moment that the two of them were on public display.

"I like what you're doing," he said as she returned to her work, filling the scene with the small details that would add up to a total story. "I mean throughout the store," he amended.

"Thank you," she said. "I still want to sit down with you and get a better grip on what your complete concept for the store is. Patrick and George have been very helpful, but I've always believed in going straight to the source—in this case you." She disappeared and returned momentarily with a stepladder.

"Let me do that." Josh was immediately on his feet. There was something incongruous about someone so delicate lugging around ladders.

"Thanks. I've got it. Part of the job, you know. I just want to readjust this spot. See what you think." In seconds she'd set up the ladder and scampered up, swinging one leg over the top to perch there while she used both hands to adjust the light.

Josh stood just below her. He told himself he was holding the ladder steady for her, but he was actually steadying himself as he studied her. Her body was firm and muscular, yet feminine and inviting. As feminine and inviting as the negligee she was trying to highlight. "I think it's perfect," he said hoarsely, and looked out toward the street, willing himself to break the spell of the fantasy world she was creating around them. But the cars and people outside were of little help. He could only focus on an image playing in his head of Marlo Fletcher in that negligee, in that romantic room, in that bed.

Without warning, the ladder tipped precariously as she swung her leg back and started to climb down. Josh instinctively reached up to catch her. Expertly she maintained her own balance and leaped off the ladder, steadying it with her hand as she fell against him. "Sorry, Mr. Carrington. That's one of the hazards of my work. Large ladders in too small spaces. Did I hurt you?"

Josh had to get some control. In another moment he'd have forgotten they were standing in a display window in the middle of the afternoon and pulled her to him in the kind of embrace the setting demanded. In an effort to steady his breathing and nerves, he held her shoulders, attempting to make it appear as if he were steadying her. But it was a mistake to even touch her, and he turned away immediately as if he'd been burned. "I'm fine," he said gruffly.

"Well, I think you're right about the light. Everything works." She wondered if he detected the unsteadiness in her voice.

When Josh turned back to her, she'd folded the ladder and removed it from the window. Then she gathered their tea things and rinsed them quickly in a bucket of water she'd brought in. She dried the service and set it to await the two lovers, for now there was no question in Josh's mind that's whom she meant to occupy this room.

"Well, I've taken enough of your time." Josh cleared his throat and moved toward the door. "I just wanted to welcome you to the store and thank you for helping us in this emergency."

"As I said, I'd really appreciate the opportunity to sit down and discuss your ideas. For however long I'm here, it's important that Carrington's not lose ground."

It was totally unexpected. He'd never have thought her capable of understanding the business end of running the store. He realized that she had a maturity, a professionalism about her that belied her charming directness. "I'd like that very much," he said, and returned to offer her a firm handshake. "It's a pleasure to have you on staff, Ms. Fletcher." He hesitated over her title, uncertain of what to call her. Suddenly her marital status was of the deepest interest to him.

She returned his handshake and grinned with mischief. "It's...Marlo, okay?" She wondered whether she'd read his real question. If so, she wasn't going to give him an answer.

He repeated her name and released her hand. "Have a pleasant evening, Marlo."

By the time Josh made his way back to his office, it was closing time. His secretary had left for the day, and there was a message on his desk that Clare Thompson had called. Recently he'd been seeing Clare, the latest in the long line of women his mother considered to be boring companions. He felt that was unfair to Clare. She was a classic beauty in the country club manner—blond, blue-eyed, regal and rich. She was also extremely bright and had just joined her father's new law firm as a junior partner. But his mother was right; she was also predictable. With Clare, there would be no element of surprise.

On the other hand, Marlo Fletcher was anything but predictable, as he'd discovered in one short day. He was sure his mother would approve if he decided to invite Marlo to the symphony committee dinner. The idea made him smile as he gathered the daily receipts, the balance sheets and the computer printouts, and put them into his worn leather briefcase to work on at home.

He'd just eased his silver Volvo into the traffic on Prospect Avenue when he spotted Marlo striding along. Her movement was unmistakable. Who else would face the end of the day with the same energy and anticipation with which most people struggled to start it? Clearly Marlo was a woman who savored life, every minute of it. She'd added a short red wool coat to her outfit, and her cap of dark hair was hidden beneath a jaunty felt fedora. While others warily huddled at bus stops or shuffled toward their cars, Marlo moved among them as if her day were just beginning and held the promise of something exciting.

Josh realized he'd practically slowed to a crawl trying to keep her in sight. He was beginning to get some angry looks and impatient messages from other drivers, who were anxious to be home and warm. He thought of offering her a ride; after all, they were going to the same address. But he caught himself. He was acting like a smitten schoolboy, he realized. He knew he wouldn't stop for any other employee.

Since the disastrous liaison between his father and a store employee some years before, his grandfather had warned him often about the pitfalls of combining business with pleasure. The results of office entanglements too often were painful for not only the people involved but the business as well. With a sigh he reined in his fantasies about the lovely Ms. Fletcher and proceeded up the avenue at a normal speed. But more than once that night he caught himself pausing by his window to study the warm glow of light that fell across the lawn from the apartment above the carriage house.

# Three

———

Marlo had always liked working late. On Thursday nights, when the store stayed open until nine, most of the buyers and managerial staff left at five and she had the office to herself. It was quiet, and there were no interruptions or telephone calls. It was a good time to develop her ideas for the spring opening. She'd spent most of the day wandering through the store, making sketches and rough floor plans and getting ideas from the department heads and buyers. She enjoyed talking to the people who made the business run so smoothly. She knew that at first she'd been met with skepticism. The employees were loyal to George and dubious of her ability to take on his job. But she'd won many of them over, and now, more often than not, she was approached by members of the staff anxious to share an idea with her.

It was hard to believe she'd already been away from New York for nearly a month. Especially that she'd spent that time in Milwaukee—Chicago maybe, but Milwaukee? "Who'd have thought it?" she mused aloud.

Her brothers and sisters teased her whenever they called or wrote. Her brother-in-law Dan had even sent her a newspaper article about the warning signs of frostbite. Her mother, on the other hand, was far more interested in news of Josh Carrington and had kept Marlo on the phone for nearly an hour the day Marlo had told her of their initial meeting in the Victorian boudoir window.

"He sounds wonderful," Lucy Fletcher had said. "Perhaps in the spring the two of you might come out and let us meet him. Or we could come there. Where's the closest airport, dear? Chicago?"

"Milwaukee has an airport, Mom—jet planes and everything, just like other big cities."

Actually she was growing rather fond of the city. It had a small-town feeling, yet she was just beginning to appreciate how much there was to do. The theater was first-class, all the way from the road companies of the Broadway shows that stopped at the Riverside, to the local top-notch Repertory Theater and the numerous smaller companies that struggled to stay afloat. As soon as the spring promotions were successfully launched, she planned to contact every company in hopes of a guest designing spot. Of course, most designers were lined up before the season began, but . . .

Filling in her design with color, Marlo thought back to her initial meeting with her current employer. Since their afternoon tea in the window two days earlier, she'd seen Josh only fleetingly as they went about their separate business. He was always cordial, calling her by name and commenting on her work or taking interest in her personal comfort.

But Marlo had noticed that he was the same with every employee, from the buyers to the maintenance crew. He called everyone by name and seemed to know the complete personal and family history of each one. That very afternoon she'd heard him inquire about the sick husband of an employee—and he'd even known the names of her grandchildren. Marlo decided that his compassion was one of the most attractive things about him.

As he'd said no more about getting together to discuss his plans for the store since their first meeting, Marlo had con-

cluded that her brand of New York directness was a bit too
brash for this conservative Midwesterner. But she was still very
anxious to have the meeting, for a number of reasons.

"I'm more than a little out of my element here in retailing,"
she'd told Patrick one afternoon.

"You're doing great," he'd replied. "I can't believe how
quickly you're learning the business."

"Still, I'd like to discuss certain aspects of that business with
Carrington himself. No offense, Patrick, but whatever role you
might play in the store's development, it's clearly second to
Joshua's. This is a one-man show, and you can't tell me that
when we move into this big spring to-do, all designs and plans
aren't going to need clearance with the man himself. I need to
know his ideas before I can carry my own designs much further."

"I get the message," Patrick had said. "Just be a little pa-
tient. I promise it'll happen." Two days had passed since then,
and still nothing.

And then there was the man himself. As Patrick had pre-
dicted, he fascinated her. Not because of his good looks, although she had to admit that he was very handsome. Beyond
that, however, he was so quiet and reserved. He always seemed
to hold back and wait. And he was so incredibly...straight.
She'd frequently found herself wondering if the man had ever
just let go and been wildly uninhibited. Somehow that didn't
seem likely. She tried to imagine him in college with Patrick and
found the idea preposterous. She knew that Patrick had breezed
through on his exceptional intelligence and his infamous high
jinks. She'd heard some unbelievable stories of the pranks he'd
staged, and somehow she couldn't see Joshua Carrington III in
that picture.

She just couldn't seem to place him in any category.

Just yesterday she and Sally had been having lunch together
in the store's small restaurant when they'd overheard two store
buyers going on and on about Josh Carrington. With a smile,
Sally had whispered to Marlo, "Half the saleswomen in the
store have a crush on my son. And the other half spend their
breaks plotting a match for their dark, mysterious employer.
Perhaps it's those bedroom eyes he inherited. I know they were

my downfall when his father used them on me." A question mark had seemed to hang in the air, as if Sally'd been waiting for Marlo to admit to her own vulnerability to those eyes.

Perhaps it *was* his brooding eyes, Marlo thought now as she sat in the office. She found herself lightly sketching his features as she tried to recall what had given her the impression that he was somehow vulnerable and lonely. His mouth, wide, with a full lower lip, was part of that portrait. His smile came so rarely that there was hardly a trace of laugh lines that would ordinarily crease the face of a man of Josh's age. His cheekbones were high, giving his face a strength that was emphasized by the square firmness of his chin.

She penciled his dark hair, which covered the tops of his ears. Marlo recalled the childhood pictures she'd found in her apartment and smiled, wondering if he'd adopted the style because he was still sensitive about that part of his anatomy. No matter, it'd been the right choice. His hairstyle, cut in layers that swept back from his high forehead, gave him just the right look of distinction and elegance for a man who headed a high-fashion department store such as Carrington's.

Totally engrossed now, Marlo completed the powerful neck and started to outline the wide, muscular shoulders she'd noticed as she'd watched him make his way through the store in his well-tailored suits. She was musing about what those shoulders might be like beneath the always correct jacket, even beneath the always immaculate starched shirt, when a sound at the door startled her.

"May I help you?" Marlo called out, quickly burying the sketch under the pile of drawings she'd made for the spring promotions.

"Well, at least you're beginning to get the lingo down," Joshua Carrington said lightly, but the smile was less than sincere. In his charcoal suit, white shirt and perfectly knotted tie, he looked tired but still very much in control. Marlo had an urge to loosen the tie and open his collar. She was appalled to see that his hair was actually mussed, as if he'd recently run his fingers through it in exasperation. The smudges under his eyes were deeper, and there was the hint of a beard along his firm jaw. In his exhaustion he seemed eminently more approachable than ever before.

"Are you aware, Ms. Fletcher, that this establishment has been closed for half an hour?"

Marlo glanced at the watch she'd placed on the drafting table. "Really? I lost track," she said, gathering her sketches into the worn portfolio that was her constant companion. "I'm sorry to have kept you. Fred usually tells me when he's ready to lock up." Josh had moved toward the drafting table, and as she collected her scattered notes and drawings, she couldn't avoid brushing against him. She found this contact more unnerving than she would've been willing to admit.

"Are you taking work home?" he asked, indicating the bulging portfolio.

Marlo shrugged. "Occupational habit. We theater people tend to be night owls. We do our best work in the wee hours of the morning. What about you?" She nodded toward the briefcase he carried and was rewarded by a slight smile.

"Apparently retailing and show business have more in common than I thought. What time did you come in this morning?"

"Nine o'clock. Why?"

His expression was serious as he pulled a sketch from the pile she'd left on her desk. "I think a twelve-and-a-half-hour day is above the call of duty. Your boss must be a real slave driver. What are you working on here, anyway?"

"Some ideas for the spring windows—very rough ideas. Just doodles and dreams at this stage." She took the sketch and added it to the others in her portfolio.

"I'd like to hear about those dreams." He spoke quietly as he watched her bend to pull the zipper closed around the portfolio's worn leather.

"That won't be possible until you can find the time to tell me your plans for where you expect this business to be by spring." Marlo faced him as she pulled on her coat.

"You're very direct, aren't you?"

"Well, you know what they say about New Yorkers." She grinned at him, hoping to take the sharpness from her accusation.

"I like New York," he said apropos of nothing. He was looking at her hair, and she had the sudden impression that he wanted to touch her. Then the moment passed and he was all business. "I'm sorry I haven't called that meeting. I've thought about it a great deal in the past few days," he said, and added silently to himself, And you. I've thought a lot about you.

"No problem," Marlo replied. "How about now?"

"Now?"

"Well, since obviously neither of us is finished for the day—" she grinned, nodding toward her portfolio and his briefcase "—what do you say we take a break and share some coffee, conversation and chocolate decadence?"

"Chocolate decadence?"

She studied him closely until to her delight, he became distinctly uncomfortable under her scrutiny. "You know, Mr. Joshua Carrington the Third, you have some definite gaps in your education, and I gather that what's missing is a degree in fun. If you and I have any hope of working together on the same wavelength, I'm going to have to start doing something about that tonight. Get your coat, boss. I'm taking you out for coffee."

"And a little decadence?" Again she could detect just the hint of a smile.

"That's it. I can see you're going to be a very good student, Mr. Carrington."

"Josh," he said as he followed her through the door.

"Josh," she repeated. He liked the way her low voice caressed the word.

Patrick had introduced Marlo to The Coffee Trader, a popular café not far from the Carrington home, during her first week in Milwaukee. It featured a full menu, with some of the most enticing desserts she'd ever seen assembled under one roof. The café's atmosphere was conducive to lingering conversations over multiple cups of coffee, and it seemed the perfect place for her to get to know Joshua Carrington better.

When they arrived, several tables were occupied, but Josh started for a somewhat secluded table in the corner. She'd stopped at the counter and ordered for both of them before he could even glance at the selections. "Two coffees of the day and two slices of chocolate decadence, please."

While their order was being filled, Josh asked, "How do you know what the coffee of the day is?"

"What does it matter? If it's terrible, we'll order something else. And if it's great, think what we'll have discovered."

After she and Josh were settled at the table, Marlo watched him taste the chocolate confection before him. She smiled as first an expression of surprise, then one of pure pleasure, passed over his face. "That's very rich—I believe 'sinfully rich' is the description."

Marlo laughed. "I know. It really is great—you can almost feel your teeth rotting. Isn't it fun?"

"Lesson number one?"

Marlo nodded, glad to hear the slightly teasing tone in Josh's deep voice. Then she attacked her own dessert. She practically inhaled it and looked up to find Josh watching her with some fascination. His own piece was basically intact, with only one or two bites missing. "I like to savor something as rich as this," he said, though he didn't sound apologetic.

Mentally Marlo groaned. She must look completely unsophisticated at this stage, and she was beginning to realize that their different approaches to life might become a real problem in their work relationship. She tended to burst into a project from several different directions at once. Her attitude was "If this doesn't work, something else will." She could see that his own methodology was more likely to be one of thinking out every detail in advance, considering for hours, and perhaps days, the possibilities and pitfalls of every decision.

"How do you like Milwaukee?" he asked, interrupting her stream of thought.

"It's not bad," she answered, watching the barest smile fight to break the corners of his soft lips. "High praise from a native New Yorker, right? Well, other than this weather, it really does have a great deal to offer. In fact, I think what you have here is a very well-kept secret—sophistication living side by side with small-town values and even a sort of rural spirit."

"But you wouldn't choose it as a place to live?" Josh was surprised at the importance he attached to whatever she answered.

"Probably not." Had she imagined a flicker of disappointment crossing his face, or had that been disapproval? she wondered. "Oh, I might apply sometime for a guest designer's position here—you have terrific theater companies for a city of this size, you know."

"Thank you. You'll have to tell that to my mother—she's on the boards of several groups. But then, you know that already, don't you?"

"Your mother is a delightful lady, Josh." Marlo leaned across the table. Her instinct was to take his hand, but she reached for her coffee instead. By nature she was a person who touched and hugged other people spontaneously. "I suppose your family is involved in many civic projects. I'm sure that's good for business."

"It is, but in my mother's case she'd pay *them* for the privilege of working in the theater. She's a former actress. Did she tell you?"

"She did. I found the whole idea mind-boggling. I mean, your family hardly seems—whoops, I'm sure that sounded completely tactless!"

"Is it really so surprising? Even people in Milwaukee aspire to the arts, you know."

"Oh, I know. Some of the best in the world are from this area. It's just that—well, it doesn't matter. I'd like to meet the rest of your family. Is your mother at all active in running the store?"

That brought the first genuinely open laugh she'd ever heard from him. "Mother?" No, she stays as far away from the store as possible."

"And your grandfather?"

The smile left his face. "It's my grandfather's store—he founded it. Unfortunately he's recently had a battle with arthritis and the aftermath of a stroke to contend with. The illnesses have left him in a wheelchair, and he hasn't been down to the store since ... my father died." He sipped his coffee. "This is very good," he said, and drank some more.

Marlo waited for him to continue to talk about his family, but he remained silent. She tried another tack. "Patrick tells me this whole spring campaign is predicated on reintroducing the store to the public as it was in those early days." Perhaps if she stayed on the safer ground of business she could get off this roller coaster, which kept her so unsure of his reactions.

He leaned forward eagerly. "You know, Marlo, when Carrington's first opened, it had an excellent reputation. We handled only the finest merchandise, and people would make a special trip downtown just to look at our window displays. Carrington's was *the* fashion authority in the state."

"What happened?" He was talking about a time years before his birth as if he'd witnessed it himself. She was spellbound.

"For thirty years it got better and better. We weathered the Depression, when stores across the country were going bankrupt. And during the war years, we were able to maintain our high standards in spite of the shortages. In the fifties it was a boom time all over again—parties, debuts, weddings...."

"And then?" Marlo asked softly, afraid that if she became too intrusive he'd finish his narration in a couple of sentences and be done. She felt as if she were on the brink of learning something important about this man.

"And then came the sixties." Again the silence and withdrawal.

"Josh?" This time she covered his hand with hers.

"Retailing changed in the sixties and seventies, Marlo. The discounting concept took the country by storm, and it became the way to go, especially with the state of the economy. Add to that the fact that high fashion is hard to sell when it's unfashionable to be seen in anything but jeans and a T-shirt. Carrington's adapted to the times.

"Actually, my father had no choice. We added more racks, more lines in the lower ranges. We went after every customer we could get. In those days departments came and went so fast, it was hard to know from one week to the next what would be in the store and where it would be. Bell-bottoms were in, so we carried bell-bottoms—no matter how hideous they looked on most women. The mini, the midi—whatever Seventh Avenue dictated. We carried whatever everyone else did, for fear of losing a customer if we didn't have the stock.''

The tired look had returned and settled into short vertical lines that cut deep furrows between his brows. He looked discouraged and pressured.

"And where are we headed in the eighties?" she asked, hoping that talking of the future would cheer him.

"Unless the bank has a little more imagination, we may be heading out of business." He was stroking the back of her hand absently with his thumb, and she liked the closeness she was feeling at the moment. Suddenly he pulled his hand away and looked at her as if he'd just realized she was there. "That's certainly not for further discussion with anyone beyond this table," he warned her.

"Of course not," she replied. "But surely it isn't as bad as all that. You've got some very good lines in the store now—I certainly wouldn't call it a bargain basement. You're even carrying some lines I haven't found anywhere else in town."

"That's five years of hard work you're seeing. Five years of mostly seven days a week and sixteen-hour days to make up for twenty years of benign neglect from my father. It might not be enough. I can't see how we can pull this off by March."

"But that's all the more reason why we should talk, Josh. I need to know what I can do to help. I know George's heart attack couldn't have come at a worse time, but at least let me try."

He was touched by her concern. "George is certainly one of the best, but don't get the idea that I'm not aware of your considerable talents. From what I've seen, we're very lucky Patrick made that trip to New York."

"But you weren't sure at first, were you?" She was smiling now.

"I'll admit I had my doubts. I've spent five years assembling a staff of the best retail people I could get. I wasn't interested in taking any steps backward, and that's how I viewed hiring anyone from outside retailing. Fortunately for me, Patrick didn't mention you. He just hired you, knowing you'd work your magic on the store, and then told me to go have a look. Patrick certainly has a way of cutting through red tape."

"Careful there. You might actually give me a full-blown grin." She studied his lips and eyes.

In place of the smile she'd hoped for, the lines came together in a frown. "You make me sound like some sort of solemn ogre."

"Well, solemn fits. Not an ogre, though. Definitely not that."

He relaxed his face and leaned toward her. "Marlo, I do owe you some thanks. You've already brought a fresh look to the store with just the routine midwinter changes. I can hardly wait to see what you're planning for spring. Are you aware that up and down the avenue, people are buzzing about the new look at Carrington's? It's more than I'd hoped for at this stage."

She twirled an imaginary mustache and said in a conspiratorial whisper, "So I've passed the initiation and now you'll admit me to the inner circle, where I'll learn of your secret plans."

She was pleased when he smiled openly at her. "You've got it. Come to my office in the morning and I'll show you the whole concept."

"Speaking of tomorrow, we'd better get out of here. We both have those bulging briefcases, remember?"

"I forbid you to do another bit of work today, Ms. Fletcher." He stood and helped her with her coat. His hands hovered at her shoulders for a moment, and he was surprised at the urge he felt to pull her against him. He was momentarily mesmerized by the shine of her short dark hair and by the scent of her woodsy perfume, which caressed her and the air around her. When she glanced over her shoulder to see why he'd made no further movement to leave, there was a question in her deep blue eyes.

Josh cleared his throat and reached for his briefcase at the same moment she picked up her portfolio. For that instant they were as close as a kiss, and neither seemed capable of moving. "Well," Josh said in a husky voice, then cleared his throat again as he straightened and stood back to allow her to pass.

They walked the block to his car in silence. He held the door for her as she stored their things in the back seat. It was a frosty night, but the car seemed inordinately warm and close. The scent of her perfume filled him with a desire he recognized as having been suppressed too long, for the sake of getting his business back on its feet.

So that was it. She was a damned attractive woman, and he'd been denying himself for some time. It could've been Clare or anyone else. But he knew he was deceiving himself. Clare's perfume didn't cause him to forget his mission. Her body didn't inspire him to have sensual fantasies in the middle of the day. Her eyes didn't entice him to explore their depths. For once he was thankful for a stick-shift car—it kept his hands busy as he pulled into the sparse traffic and headed for home.

Marlo studied his hand, which was wrapped around the gearshift. She was surprised at the strength and tenseness in his body, as if the shift were something to be struggled with and overpowered. She moved her gaze up his arm past the set of his shoulders to his face. He wore a slight scowl, which seemed an almost permanent expression. How was she going to create an atmosphere of fun and fantasy for this man's business, when the man himself was so imprisoned by ledgers and balance sheets? she wondered.

He heard her sigh and glanced at her. Thinking he was already worrying about the upcoming March opening, she lightly squeezed his arm. "We'll get it done, Josh, and we'll get it done right, so stop worrying. You should be enjoying this. Rebuilding a business into something as fine as you have at Carrington's is something you should savor."

She saw him relax his shoulders slightly but at the same time felt his arm tense under her hand. She couldn't know that her touch had fueled feelings he was loath to allow until the business was firmly on its feet again.

He pulled up the car next to the stairs that led to her apartment above the carriage house. "Well," she said, confused by his reactions to her, "see you tomorrow."

He cut the engine and walked around to open the car door for her. As he helped her out of the car and reached into the back seat for her portfolio, she studied him for an instant before allowing her natural directness to rule the moment.

"Josh, I wish I'd known you in those days when Patrick first did, when you were a carefree kid whose greatest worry was whether you'd be suspended for some prank the two of you had pulled. If you were free right now to do whatever you wanted, I wonder what would that be.''

He looked at her for a long moment, and she thought he was trying to formulate an answer.

"Don't think about it—stop analyzing everything. Just gut reaction. What would you do?'' She'd taken a step closer when he handed her her portfolio, and her dark eyes challenged his, daring him for one moment to permit himself to throw duty to the winds.

"This," he said, and pulled her into the strong circle of his arms, using one hand to tilt her face back to receive his kiss.

Marlo was more than a little surprised, and her initial reaction was to tense in his arms, but she couldn't deny the pleasure that coursed through her as his mouth covered hers and he invited her response with his soft, full lips. And respond she did. In an instant she wrapped her arms around his neck, pulling him closer until she could feel the length of him pressed against her body. Her toes barely touched the ground as she stretched to match his taller frame. In the next moment she felt him opening her coat to draw her firmly against his chest and at the same time felt the tip of his tongue as he sought entry into her mouth. She opened to him, exulting in this first display of passion for something other than his business.

She wound her fingers through his thick hair. When he pulled away a moment later, she was delighted with the curls and tendrils that had fallen over his forehead. They gave him a boyish charm she'd suspected since the day the two of them had first talked in her Victorian window. She opened her eyes and met his. "You're not smiling," she teased him.

"Oh, yes I am," he replied, stone-faced. Then he gave her a slight push toward the stairs. He watched until she was safely inside.

She heard his car move into the garage and the crunch of his footsteps on the snow-packed driveway as he walked to the main house.

After working for another couple of hours on the plans she hoped to show him soon, she stretched her muscles, then wandered through the apartment. From her bedroom she had the

best view of the main house and the solitary amber light she'd
noticed her first night there. It had to be Josh's room or study.
She saw his silhouette in the high arched window and knew that
he was gazing back. In that moment it was almost as if he'd
touched her again.

# Four

The following morning Marlo wasn't surprised to find Patrick waiting with Joshua for their appointment. Josh was basically shy, a quality that only endeared him more to Marlo. She knew that his kissing her the night before had been totally out of character, and she'd expected him to express some doubt about his wisdom in having taken such a risk.

"Patrick," she said, extending her hand to him. Then she turned and leaned across the desk to shake Joshua's hand. "Good morning, Mr. Carrington." Her eyes flashed with good humor as she dared him with a look to deny that he'd called Patrick to this meeting merely as a safety net. Joshua had the good grace to color slightly as he returned her handshake.

"Since the three of us will be working closely together over the coming weeks, I believe we can dispense with such formalities. It's Josh, remember?"

Her smile widened. "Oh, I remember," she replied deliberately, giving a double entendre to her answer. She was rewarded by a slight smile, one that reached his dark eyes this time.

Patrick looked curiously from one to the other and cleared his throat loudly as if to remind them he was still in the room. "Am I interrupting a private joke?"

"Not at all, Patrick. Marlo and I were just laying some ground rules." He gave her a full smile and turned to the wall calendar behind his desk. "Now, if you'll both step over here, I'll fill Marlo in on our plans."

Marlo was surprised to see that he could give as good as he got from her. He might be shy, but she could tell that when baited, Joshua Carrington could deliver a few surprise punches of his own. He proved it now by slipping one arm around her waist, ostensibly to guide her around his desk to study the calendar. But Marlo felt the color rise in her cheeks at his touch, and she didn't miss the glimmer of triumph that lit his eyes as he began to discuss the deadlines and plans.

The intercom buzzed and they heard Wilma ask Patrick to take a call from the local newspaper.

"I'd better handle this in my office, where I have all the details. Be back as soon as I can. You two go ahead," he said as he started for the door.

For several minutes after Patrick had left, Joshua spoke with excitement about the work they'd already accomplished. "But it all comes together here," he said, tapping a red-circled date in March with his forefinger. "This is D-Day, and we'd better be ready or we'll have gambled and lost. It's got to be a dynamic promotion, Marlo," he finished.

He stood for a minute, glaring at the calendar, and then turned to get her reaction. He was surprised when he looked down to find her grinning widely, as if he'd just awarded her the Tony for best design.

When she saw his surprise, she knew his mood bordered on irritation because he thought she wasn't taking this whole project seriously enough. This was his life and she was smiling. "Hold it," she warned him, moving back around the desk to open her portfolio. "I know how important this is, but I just realized that with George's help we're definitely on the right track in display. Come around here and let me show you some ideas." She might have added that Marlo Fletcher loved putting on a show and he'd just handed her one that would be as much fun as any play she'd ever designed. She couldn't wait to get started.

For the next hour she dazzled him with one idea after another. Some were rejected as being too close to what had been done by others. Others they decided were a bit too avant-garde for Milwaukee. The ideas that appealed most to Joshua were those that played on Carrington's role in the history of the city. "Okay. Let me take these three and expand on them and then you can make a final choice," she said after they'd debated on each idea.

"We don't have the time to develop three concepts—we hardly have the time to develop one properly," Joshua said doubtfully, and she noticed how he combed his fingers through his hair in frustration. "I may have cut it too close. Perhaps by fall we'd be better prepared."

"As I understand it," Marlo said quietly as he paced the office, "you don't have that luxury. Would Monday morning be too late to reconsider these three ideas in their expanded forms and make a final selection?"

Joshua looked at her as if she'd just announced she planned to walk on the ceiling. "What are you going to do—work around the clock?"

She held his eyes and nodded. "If that's what it takes." And then she winked, breaking into a smile that lit her whole face. "Might as well get used to it, Carrington. From what I can see, the three of us are going to be pulling more than one all-nighter before this is through."

She saw a wicked gleam in his eyes. "What?" She knew he'd just had a very impish thought, and she wanted him to share those thoughts with her—to let her get to know more than the businessman. "Come on, what?"

"I was just thinking that the idea of spending more than one all-nighter with you is very tempting. Is there any way we can ditch Patrick?"

She laughed and shook her head. "Not if you want these ideas worked up by Monday morning."

"Okay, Monday morning." Marlo could hear the skepticism in his tone.

"I can do it, Josh. I really can." She touched his arm in a gesture of reassurance.

When he looked down at her, it seemed as if he might kiss her, and she realized that was what she wanted. Business was forgotten as without the buffer of Patrick's presence the two of them allowed their kiss of the previous night to play itself out across their minds and faces.

"I'm sure you can do it, Marlo," he whispered in a hoarse voice, framing her face in his hands. "I'm beginning to think there's a great deal you can do for me that has nothing to do with business."

She was in his arms instantly, and her hunger was all-consuming. He let his hands rove over her slight body as he brought his mouth down on hers. The attraction they'd held in check since their first meeting exploded, and the businesslike mood disappeared as she burrowed her hands under his jacket to trace the hard muscular contours of his back and shoulders. Marlo couldn't get close enough to him, and if his holding and kissing her was any barometer, the feeling was mutual.

He whispered her name against her ear, hugging her tightly while they attempted to catch their breath.

"I know," she said. "Me, too."

She took a step away and had just straightened her clothing when Patrick burst into the room.

"Great news—" He stopped by the door. Clearly he saw that he'd interrupted something. He half turned to leave, muttering something about coming back later.

"What news?" Josh asked, striding back to his desk and busying himself with his papers.

"*The Journal*'s Lifestyle section is planning a Sunday feature on J.P. and the reopening of the store for their spring fashion edition—color pictures, multiple stories, the works!"

"That's fantastic," Marlo offered. "Isn't it great, Josh?" She risked a look at him. His eyes didn't hide the fact that he still wanted her.

"Fantastic," he repeated, but she knew he wasn't speaking of Patrick's news. Then, clearing his throat, he straightened and turned to the calendar, adding the date of the feature to the list of promotional plans.

"Come on, Patrick, we've got work to do," Marlo said, gathering her portfolio and sketches and tugging at his sleeve. "I'll give you the rundown as we walk. I'll need all your ideas and the deadlines and delivery dates for ads and promos, not to mention the merchandise you're expecting. Do you have artwork on the designer lines yet?"

"Could we have time to pick up a cup of coffee, slave driver?" Patrick was right beside her, his arm casually draped around her slim shoulder. "By the way, kiddo, what are your plans for the weekend?"

"Same as yours—working. Now, come on."

Joshua made polite conversation with a violinist through the first course, but by the time the salad arrived, he was thankful his dinner partner had turned to chat with the person on her left. He accepted his mother's not-too-subtle eye signals that this was important for him and the store. But his mind wasn't on the elegant dinner party. In fact, it was back at the store. Not that his mother would have found that unusual. But had she known his mind was not on business but rather on a certain petite brunette with the deepest blue eyes he'd ever seen, she would have been downright shocked, not to mention thrilled.

His grandfather was another story. The older man sat at the head of the table, charming the chairwoman of the symphony board and occasionally casting questioning looks at his only heir with equal aplomb.

Joshua loved and admired the older man tremendously. J. P. Carrington had in many ways been his father, and Josh had intended to follow in his grandparent's footsteps for as long as he could remember. He'd looked forward to working in the store under the founder's guidance. But then there had been the stroke and the debilitating arthritis, not to mention the crippling scandal of his father's affair with a store employee. J.P. had emerged from the last decade disappointed and frequently embittered. Joshua knew his grandfather loved him, but he also knew that after the experience of having a son who cared nothing for the store, the older man was less than enthusiastic about the idea of having anyone but himself in control of the business he'd built from scratch.

So for the past five years, Joshua had spent just about every waking hour trying to win the trust and support of his grandfather, trying to restore the business to what it had once been, making that restoration the portrait of the love and esteem he felt for the older man. But tonight his heart just wasn't in it. The dinner was boring. More than ever he wanted to be at the store, making plans, brainstorming ideas with Patrick and Marlo. He wanted to be with her.

Clare smiled at him from across the table, completely without annoyance that he'd invited her at the last minute. Josh had intended to invite Marlo until she'd announced her intention to work, and once again his loyalty to the mission he'd set for the store won out over his personal life. In the past several months he'd asked Clare anytime he needed a date, and he knew that he was leaving her with the wrong impression about their relationship.

He'd played the field for several years, but she'd been his almost constant companion since his father had died. Everyone thought the shock of the death had made him want to settle down and assumed he and Clare would marry. He should've found a way before now to explain that their relationship was more a matter of convenience than grand passion. Not that Clare wasn't attractive—she was actually quite lovely, as well as bright, and perfect in the role of hostess for events like this dinner. But when he kissed or held her, there was no longing in him—no desire to prolong the contact.

That could hardly be said of his kisses with Marlo. Those impulsive acts were beginning to stack up as one of his major missteps in a long time. He hadn't been able to do a bit of work after leaving her the night before. Instead, he'd stood at his window, staring out at the lights in the carriage house. And this afternoon at the store, he'd caught himself daydreaming about her. The meeting in his office had very nearly been a fiasco. Until she'd begun to reel off her ideas for the spring campaign, he'd been unable to concentrate on anything but her presence in the room. Then once she'd finished and he'd seen her incredible talent and enthusiasm in action, he hadn't been able to keep his hands off her. If Patrick hadn't come in . . .

"Excuse me?" He was jolted from his reverie by a comment from his dinner partner. Obviously the first violinist was repeating herself. He caught his grandfather's raised eyebrows and gave his undivided attention to getting through the rest of the evening without another lapse.

After he had driven Clare home, Joshua sat with the old man in the library, something they did at the end of the day whenever possible. Dressed for bed, his grandfather sat in his wheelchair near the large bay windows, sipping his nightly brandy. "Brandy, Joshua?"

"No, thank you, sir." J.P. knew Josh never drank brandy, but he often assumed his heir would share his preferences. Joshua hoped that soon he would prove to his grandfather that while their tastes might differ, they were of the same stock when it came to the more basic things of life.

"Interesting evening, don't you think?" The older man's tone was entirely neutral. Joshua wondered whether he only imagined the undercurrents in his grandfather's most innocent conversations.

"I don't know. I found it fairly predictable."

"You did seem a bit preoccupied. Is there a problem with the store?"

J. P. Carrington had turned the reins over to his grandson after his son's death, saying, "If you wish to run Carrington's, Joshua, you'll have to go it alone. You'll have to rescue this ship your father so blithely allowed to sink in the sea of scandal and fiscal irresponsibility." After that he'd withdrawn all monetary support and never mentioned the store unless the subject was brought up by someone else.

And Joshua had taken charge. He'd emptied his own bank accounts and poured money into the business. And every night that he could, he came and sat with his grandfather in the library and quietly filled him in on his efforts. Occasionally he solicited the older man's advice directly. More often he simply spelled out a particular problem and then waited. Within a few days his grandfather would offer Josh some advice, tossing it off as if it were an afterthought. His question tonight was the first direct reference to the business he'd made in five years, and

Josh, seeing it as a sign of faith in what he was doing, was pleased.

"There's no problem," he said, meeting his grandfather's steady gaze, then smiled. "At least not one we haven't already discussed."

They were silent for a time, staring into the fire. After a while J.P. said, "What about this young woman you've hired to handle the merchandising? Your mother seems quite taken with her. From New York, is she?"

He glanced at his grandfather's studiously casual expression. "I see your sources have been busy," Josh teased him gently. "What would you like to know about her? Or, more to the point, what don't you know already?"

There was a pause during which the old man studied him for a long moment. And then, as if he'd come to a decision, he launched into his answer. "I don't know why my grandson, who seemed to be heading in exactly the right direction to pull off the business revitalization of the decade, would hire a mere woman to handle merchandising. I don't know why, even if he had to entrust such an important position to a woman, he would choose someone with not one day's experience in retailing." His eyes were bright and alert and steely gray as he challenged Joshua to answer.

The two men were startled from their debate by the throaty voice of Sally Carrington. "Joshua Porterfield Carrington, when are you going to move into the twentieth century?" She moved easily into the room, then helped herself to a sherry at the bar and settled cross-legged on the floor in front of the fire. "A 'mere woman' could be just the ticket for pulling off this coup you and my son are plotting."

"Sally, my dear, we're discussing business here."

"J.P., my dear, I thought you didn't care what happened to the store. And I'll remind you that this is my business, too—your son left his shares to me, with your full approval. So come down off your patronizing high horse and let Josh tell you about Marlo."

The two of them turned expectantly toward Josh. He had to smile at the way his mother handled his grandfather. She'd been the same with him from the day she'd married into the family.

The word was that the only way to get to J. P. Carrington was to go through Sally. For all his bluster and bluff, it was clear that he delighted in her direct and unique personality. Josh recalled the day his grandfather had come home from the hospital faced with life in a wheelchair. A somewhat dramatic man, he'd spent several days taking his meals in his room, then came into the dining room one evening and announced to the assembled family that since he'd been sentenced to die in that damnable chair, it was time they discussed his will and plans for the funeral.

While the teenaged Josh and his father had laid their forks aside in shock, Sally had calmly continued to eat her dinner. Without missing a beat she'd firmly told J.P., "Nonsense. You'll outlive most of us. You've only been given a new way of mobility. If you choose to die in that chair, it's hardly our business. Please come to the table before your soup gets any colder."

Now Josh looked at the two of them as they waited for his answer. "From everything I've seen of her work, I think Marlo Fletcher is perfectly capable of handling merchandise whether or not George comes back."

"George will be back. Those artistic types tend to overdramatize everything. It's only a heart attack, you know." J.P.'s gruffness belied his concern for an old and favored employee. Josh knew his grandfather had made several visits to the hospital and that he'd telephoned George on those days he wasn't up to visiting.

"Nevertheless," Josh continued, "he won't be back in time for the spring campaign. Patrick was able to contact Marlo and bring her here. We're very lucky she was between jobs in New York just then."

"'Between jobs'...such a quaint way these theater types have of saying 'out of work.'" J.P. caught Sally's look and didn't continue.

"This morning Patrick and I met with Marlo, and she outlined a number of proposals for the theme of the spring opening. We settled on three possibilities. Right now she and Patrick are working out the details for a presentation Monday afternoon."

"Oh, so that's why she wasn't with you at dinner tonight, dear. I was sure you were going to bring her and was surprised when you arrived with Clare. Not that Clare isn't perfectly lovely—but then that's a bit of a problem with Clare, isn't it? She's so perfectly everything. I honestly live for the day she has a hair out of place," Sally mused as she sipped her sherry.

"You're seeing Miss Fletcher socially, Joshua?" The disapproval was undisguised in the old man's expression, although his tone remained very controlled and conversational. The unwritten law that Carringtons didn't mix business with pleasure hung in the air. His own son had proved that breaking it was an invitation to disaster.

"Well, of course he's seeing her, J.P. Have you met this woman? She's so bright and vibrant. If you ask me, she'd have contributed enormously to an otherwise rather staid evening."

"Well, I'm not asking you, Sally. I'm asking my grandson."

"I'd intended to invite her to dinner, but before I had the chance, she announced her intention to work through the weekend."

"And I assume she's living in the carriage house at your invitation, Sally?"

"Oh, honestly, J.P., think of it as good for business, if nothing else. Patrick came to me and told me she needed a place to live—to sublet. She likes to walk, she doesn't have a car, and this was a *store emergency*. I felt the prudent and expedient thing to do was to rent her the carriage house."

J.P. snorted. "You're matchmaking, Sally Carrington."

"Of course I'm matchmaking. If you persist in visiting the sins of the father on your grandson, he may never find someone. The man is well into his thirties and he's alone, J.P., if you haven't noticed."

"We're not in the lonely hearts business. Joshua is hardly lacking for female companionship. That Thompson woman is perfectly—"

"Boring," Sally shouted before he had a chance to complete the sentence. "She is intelligent and beautiful and totally predictable. Josh needs some fun in his life. Since his father died, he's buried himself in that cursed business—"

"Excuse me," Josh interrupted, rising and starting for the door. "Since I've heard this particular debate before, I'll say good night. Mother." He kissed her cheek lightly. "Grandfather." He gently squeezed the older man's shoulder as he passed him on his way out.

It was after midnight by the time Patrick drove Marlo home. He was exhausted, but she was still brimming over with ideas and details, talking a mile a minute. "Now tomorrow, Patrick—"

"Tomorrow is Saturday, love. We're talking the weekend—you know, time off?"

"Not on your life." Marlo allowed him to help her out of his small sports car. "If we're going to be ready Monday, we'll be lucky if we don't have to pull at least one all-nighter."

"I thought we did, tonight." Patrick grinned.

"Come on, it's early yet. Oh, Patrick, I'm so excited about this project! I can't wait to see it all pulled together. We're going to set this city on its ear."

Patrick yawned broadly and pushed her toward the foot of the stairs that led to her apartment. "Who'd have thought you could get this excited about doing windows?" he teased her. "Now, get some sleep, or you're going to burn out just when we need you the most. You're right, kiddo. Josh is going to be impressed. But then from what I was able to gather this morning, he's already pretty impressed, and it has very little to do with your talent for retailing."

"Stop fishing, Patrick Dean. Our boss was all business this morning, as he is ninety-nine percent of the time." She pulled out her keys and started to open the heavy door.

"You don't know him well enough yet. The man was very distracted this morning, my dear—*very* distracted. There was a certain electricity in the air, if you get my drift."

"I didn't notice," Marlo said with a grin. "Do you want some coffee?" She motioned to the now open door.

"You and Josh are cut from the same mold, you know. I thought bringing the two of you together would be good, but you're both workaholics. Honestly, Marlo, you don't have to kill yourself for this job."

"I like the work," Marlo said with a shrug. "I always have. It's such pure pleasure to put all the pieces together and watch it all work. Do you want some coffee or not?"

"What I want, love, is a nice, soft bed. Get some sleep—skip the coffee." He leaned over, kissed her chastely on the cheek and left.

Marlo was inside before she realized she'd left her portfolio in the back seat of Patrick's car. She raced out to try to catch him. "Patrick!" Her voice was lost in the roar of the engine half a block away.

"Problem?"

"Joshua." She hadn't seen him, and they nearly collided on the driveway. Instantly she noticed there was something different about him, and it took her a moment to realize it was the first time she'd seen him in casual clothing. The jeans, heavy wool sweater and ski jacket did wonders for making him look approachable. "Aha," she said, grinning, "I knew all those three-piece suits and stiff collars and ties were just a ruse. Underneath there lurks a free spirit after all."

"You do have some strange ideas about me, don't you? Now I've become a Dr. Jekyll and Mr. Hyde—one persona by day and another by night." The east wind off the lake whipped his hair over his forehead, and his features were soft as he looked down at her.

"What are you doing roaming around in the middle of the night, then, if it isn't that you change personalities under a full moon?" she asked.

He smiled. "I couldn't sleep. Sometimes a walk helps me. Want to come along?"

"Sure." She fell into step with him at once as they started up the street in the clear, cold night.

"You worked very late," he commented after several minutes of silence.

"Is that a question or just an observation?"

"Both, I guess. I wasn't eavesdropping, but I overheard you and—um—Patrick." His head was down and he wasn't looking at her, but she felt him waiting for an answer.

"Joshua Carrington—" she laughed "—are you checking up on me? Is that a part of your concern for your employees? I mean, if so, I have it on good authority that Fred, the night watchman, and Bernice, from Payroll, have been seeing each other for years. Though with their different hours, I'm not sure how they pull it off."

"I'm not interested in the private lives of Bernice and Fred," he said, his voice husky.

She stopped him by pulling at his arm, forcing him to face her under the cold white light of the street lamp. "But you are interested in *my* private life?"

He studied her hungrily for a moment, and she didn't flinch from matching his look. He seemed to wrestle with an answer. Then he said, "You live in our home and work for us. You're here temporarily as a favor to my good friend Patrick. Of course we're concerned." And with that he started to walk again. He seemed to expect her to follow.

But instead she scooped a pile of the wet heavy snow into a huge snowball, which she aimed at his retreating back. She hit her mark and was delighted to see him hunch his shoulders as the wet snow found its way under the neck of his sweater and down his back. "'Of course, we're concerned,'" she mocked him. "Would that be the royal 'we,' Joshua Carrington the Third?" she shouted as she landed another direct hit to his chest just as he turned disbelievingly toward her.

"What are you," he raged as he grabbed a handful of snow and headed for her, "a pitcher for the Yankees? Stand still, Fletcher. You asked for this!" He grabbed her and anchored her firmly under one arm as he thoroughly scrubbed her face with the snow.

They were laughing as she broke away and raced down the street to a safe distance until she could fortify herself with another snowball. "Not the Yankees," she called as she lobbed one snowball after another at his advancing figure. "The Mets. Stay away from me, Carrington," she warned him. "Or I'll scream and bring the whole neighborhood down on you."

"For someone from New York," he said menacingly as he continued to stalk her, "you're very naive. If you scream in New York, do people leave their nice warm beds on a winter night to come to your aid?" He was grinning openly as he batted away her snowballs, effortlessly moving closer and closer as she continued to back away from him.

Out of ammunition, Marlo turned to run just as he reached for her, but her foot hit ice instead of pavement, and together she and Josh toppled into an ice-packed snowbank. In seconds he had her pinned and was rubbing snow into her hair and stuffing it down the front of her jacket. They were laughing like a couple of ten-year-olds playing King of the Mountain. "Uncle!" she cried, finally unable to get her breath from the laughter and the shock of the ice melting against her skin.

When she stopped struggling, Josh still didn't let her go. Instead, he stayed poised over her, his face serious after the rich, full sound of his laughter. His expression was unreadable as he knitted his thick brows together while he apparently wrestled with some private decision. She waited and watched, and when she realized his struggle was with the decision whether to kiss her, she solved his problem by kissing him first.

By the time the kiss ended, she no longer felt the chill of the snowbank—she'd become aware of the erotic position of their bodies. One of his legs was sprawled across hers. He held her pressed to the ground with one arm while he tangled his fingers in her short dark hair. His face was no more than a kiss away, and perhaps for the first time in her life, Marlo Fletcher couldn't think of one clever thing to say.

With a shake of his head, Josh rolled away and stood up, offering his hand to her. "We'd better head back," he said thickly. "You're soaked, and the last thing we need is for you to get sick." The words came out more gruffly than he'd intended them to.

Marlo sighed and thrust her hands deep into the pockets of her coat as she trudged along next to him. "We're back to that royal 'we' again, Josh."

He didn't say anything until they were back at her door. "You need to get out of those wet clothes, Marlo, and when are you going to get a decent coat? That thing wouldn't keep you warm in Florida."

"Maybe you could help me pick out a proper Wisconsin coat," she teased him, opening the door and leaving it ajar as she waited for him to follow her in. She left him no choice as she continued to talk to him while she walked through the apartment, shedding her coat and gloves and hat.

"Sure. I'll have some selections sent over here tomorrow and you can choose the one you want," he said, standing just inside the door, seemingly unsure of what his next move might be. Marlo went into the small kitchen and put on a pan of milk to warm.

"I'm making some cocoa, okay?"

Cocoa was innocent enough. "Okay," he called back, and took off his jacket and hung it on the coat tree inside the door. He walked around the room until she came from the kitchen carrying the steaming mugs.

"I don't have any marshmallows," she said with an apologetic smile.

He took the mug and followed her to the couch. "I'm sure we can make do," he offered, and wondered why every word that came out of his mouth seemed to have a double meaning.

They drank the cocoa in silence. She noticed how tired he looked. He noticed how quiet she was. They tried several topics of safe conversation and failed after one or two exchanges.

"I thought you were going to get into something dry," he said after another long silence.

"I'm afraid if I leave the room to change, you'll run away," she teased him gently.

"I'll stay for a bit, but we both do need some rest, Marlo."

She nodded and moved into the bedroom, leaving the door open and talking to him about things at the store. She was resigned to that being the only safe conversation for the evening. She got out of her clothes and turned as she belted her robe. He was standing in the doorway, watching her. The room was dark except for the light that spilled over from the living room. She couldn't see his face, but when he opened his arms, she went to him with no reservation.

Their kisses carried them the few steps from the door to the bed. In seconds he'd pushed the robe away to allow him access to her bare shoulder. Whispering her name against her skin he trailed kisses up the side of her neck to her ear.

She felt no shame or reservation at his having seen her undressed. She wanted that and knew he wanted it as well. Perhaps it was the thought that she'd be here for only a short time, but it seemed as if everything about what they felt for each other needed to be speeded up. Their attraction from the first had been leading to this moment, and she was happy it had finally come. Neither of them was inexperienced. She only hoped that in this case it meant as much to him as it did to her.

His kisses and worshipful caresses were without the reticence she'd come to expect from him. The lack of reserve delighted her, and she sought ways to encourage this free expression of what he was feeling. She unbuttoned his shirt and pulled it from his jeans. She massaged his shoulders and back until his breathing told her that he wanted more. She ran her fingers up and down the dark hair that covered his chest, and when he pressed her hips intimately into his she could feel the hard evidence of his manhood.

"Marlo," he groaned, "I want you so much. You make me feel..." He searched for the proper words and, finding none, he left it at that. "You make me feel."

Then, surprisingly, he pulled away from her, tugging at the edges of the robe to cover her.

"But...?" Her body was alive with her desire for him, and she thought she would die for the loss of his mouth on hers.

He took a deep, shuddering breath and started to put on his shirt. "But the timing is all wrong. There's too much else going on now."

She nodded, pretending to understand and fastened the robe as she walked with him into the suddenly glaring light of the living room. She let him put on his jacket. She watched as he opened the door, and she stood still while he planted a kiss on her forehead. She even let him get halfway down the stairs.

"I've never known when to keep my mouth shut, so why should tonight be an exception?" she said. She walked back down until she stood one step above him, their eyes meeting. "Look, we're two adults. Can't we just be frank about the fact that we're interested in and attracted to each other? Do you really have time to play games? Do you even want to? Oh, shut up, Marlo," she admonished herself, "and go to bed. Good night, Josh. I'll see you at the store."

When she turned to go, he caught her wrist and pulled her
back to face him. "Wait for the answers. Yes, I am attracted to
you—very attracted. No, I don't play games. And as for your
unasked question about what's going on in here..." He tapped
his forehead with two fingers. "The answer is that I'm not sure
yet. What I do know is that I can't concentrate on both the
blizzard of feelings you arouse in me and the salvation of my
business. I have to choose—no, strike that. I have no choice,
Marlo. For now, when I'm this close, the store has to be it. Do
you understand?"

She smiled, smoothing the furrows that lined his brow with
one finger. "For now, it'll have to do. But I warn you, Josh
Carrington, from what I've heard of blizzards, they have a way
of taking over and shutting down everything else." And then
she took his face between both her hands and kissed him
soundly on the forehead before turning again to run up the
stairs.

Late Monday afternoon, Josh sat silently in his office as
Marlo and Patrick presented the fruits of their marathon
weekend. They had the total package—merchandising, displays, advertising. "The key is the staff, Josh," Marlo said
when she'd presented the three separate themes for the opening festivities. "Patrick has come up with an incredible concept. The staff will be involved in a long-range extension of the
initial promotion, beginning with special training, fashion, and
makeup seminars that will aid each employee in creating the
Carrington image for himself or herself. The customer comes
into the store and sees the image all around her, and she wants
it, too."

"How do you propose we pull that one off?" Josh leaned
back in his swivel chair and steepled his fingers. His eyes never
left her face. It was impossible to read him.

"It will cost you," Patrick said. "Now, hear us out. What
we're suggesting is that you allow employees to purchase
clothing for work at a greater discount than they do now."

"How much of a discount?" Josh was suspicious.

"Cost." Patrick raised his hand against the protest he saw
coming. "With the clear understanding that the clothing is to

be worn for work and with some limits on items and numbers of pieces within each quarter. Otherwise the normal employee discount is in force.''

Marlo could see that Josh was actually considering the idea and decided to leap in. ''As a woman and as a shopper with little time, I can tell you that it'd be a blessing to find a store where I could have total confidence in the expertise of the sales staff.''

On cue Patrick drove the point home. ''You see, Josh, the key is not only having the staff look the part but in giving them the information to make the sale. Not that our staff doesn't look good now, but what we're after is a staff that presents a composite portrait of the Carrington look. And the pièce de résistance belongs to Marlo—she has an incredible idea. We could mix departments together so that accessories end up next to the dress or sportswear department, instead of two floors away. A customer tries on pants in sportswear, but now she has to go from the third floor back to the first to get a belt for those pants. She has hardly half an hour. It's too much trouble, so she forgets the belt or buys it somewhere else. With Marlo's idea, shopping ceases to be a hassle. It's a pleasure, the recreation it was meant to be.''

Marlo chimed in. ''Patrick tells me the three biggest complaints any store hears from customers is poor service, uninformed salespeople, and rude treatment. But if this works, we'll give them everything, along with the class that Carrington's was known for in the past.''

''Well?'' Patrick prodded him.

''Okay. We'll go with the twenties theme for the party. I think we can pull off the merchandising, even moving the departments around. The windows are a definite go. But this business with the staff...'' He was scowling, when Patrick and Marlo had worked so hard to earn his smiling praise.

''Look, Josh,'' Patrick began, but it was Josh's turn to stop him in midsentence.

''This business with the staff,'' he repeated, looking seriously from one to the other, ''is an absolute stroke of genius.'' And then he sat back and gave in to the laughter he'd had to hold in at the sight of their stricken faces. ''If the two of you could see your faces!'' he said through his whoops of laughter.

Marlo was stunned. She'd never seen this side of the very straight-arrow Josh Carrington. Not even the Joshua who indulged in snowball fights could match the unadulterated pleasure he was taking from this moment. "You mean, you like it?" she asked unnecessarily. "All of it?" She and Patrick had spent most of Sunday night trying to anticipate what his objections would be and trying to counter each one.

"Read my lips, you two: I love it. It's exactly right—exactly. I feel like the weight of the world has just been lifted from my shoulders, because, my friends, we're going to make it."

"I told you the woman was dynamite," Patrick interjected, enjoying the moment quietly for once.

"You did a lot—" Marlo began.

"Nope, all credit goes to you, fair lady." Patrick sat on the arm of her chair and hugged her.

"Thanks," she said softly, and was surprised when her eyes suddenly brimmed with tears. It must be exhaustion, she thought, but she knew it was more than lack of sleep. Her ideas were her stock in trade, and the selling of those ideas meant she'd succeeded in what she'd set out to do. When something she created made a project work, the feeling she got was pure pleasure. More and more she was beginning to realize that in many ways this job gave her exactly the same satisfaction her theater designing did.

"Well," Josh said, clearing his throat and beginning to gather the multitude of sketches and notes that covered his desk. "You two deserve the rest of the day off. Why don't you go out for a nice evening on the store?" Even as he spoke Josh knew that the last thing he wanted was for Marlo and Patrick to spend any more time together. After all, they were two extremely attractive people, he thought, and why shouldn't they be drawn to each other? After what he'd told her last night, there was certainly no reason Marlo should stand around waiting for him.

"Not me." Patrick took his notes and fitted them into his briefcase. "I've got a date. You two go along, though." He paused at Marlo's chair on his way out and kissed the top of her head. "Way to go, champ." He shook Josh's hand. "Are you going to tell J.P. about all this?"

Josh nodded. Patrick knew Josh told J.P. everything that had to do with the store, whether the older man showed any interest or not. They both knew that news of the business was partly responsible for keeping him going in spite of his feigned lack of interest. "He and my mom leave for Florida at the end of the week. I'll need to give him a few days to digest it all and make some comment." He smiled, knowing that Patrick understood the unspoken rules of approaching the firm's founder about the store.

"Why not let Marlo give him the rundown tonight before you two go out?" Patrick suggested.

Marlo noticed that for him there simply was no question that she and Josh would spend the evening together, but she wasn't at all sure Josh shared that idea.

"Marlo?" He studied her intently for a moment. "Yes, I think the time has come for you and my grandfather to meet. He's been wildly curious about you but far too stubborn to admit it. This is just the ticket. Could you do it?"

"I don't know." Patrick had filled her in on J. P. Carrington, as had other store employees. From what she'd been told, she didn't think he'd be overly enthusiastic about her ideas. She'd also heard the scuttlebutt about his son's infamous affair and knew that the old man would be less than thrilled to meet her if he thought she was interested in his grandson.

"It would mean a lot to me," Josh said without looking directly at her.

The man knew how to get to her. His shy demeanor could do it every time. "Okay." She was rewarded by his smile.

"Good. Come to the main house at five-thirty for cocktails. Afterward, maybe—that is, if you don't have plans—well, I mean it does seem as if a celebration is in order. Someone should say a proper thank-you for all the work you've put in. Would you go to dinner with me?"

Patrick's chuckle broke through the charged atmosphere. "Come on, Josh," he said softly. "I'm sure you can find more interesting ways to express your thanks than a simple dinner. Ciao, kids." And he was gone.

It was Marlo's turn to be unnerved. Were she and Josh so transparent? She started to fill her portfolio with the designs Josh had so neatly stacked on the corner of his large desk. She tried looking anywhere but at him until he captured her hand and held it firmly. "Where's the brash New Yorker?" he teased her, tipping her chin until she looked at him.

She smiled. "I'm just a little nervous about meeting your grandfather," she lied.

"And dinner?"

She pulled her hand free and continued to fill her portfolio. "If you're asking whether I'm nervous about having dinner with you, the answer's no. But I can't promise I'll be in any condition to eat once your grandfather finishes with me."

That brought a laugh from him. "J.P.? You have nothing to fear there, Marlo. From what I've seen of your innovative ideas, I'd better get back to the house and prepare *him*. Can I give you a lift?"

"I thought you didn't offer rides to employees—company policy?"

"It's a personal policy for me, and I'm offering you a ride to a business meeting that happens to be at my house," he replied gruffly, putting on his topcoat. "Get your things and I'll meet you in five minutes. I have to go over a couple of things with Wilma." He buzzed for his secretary.

"Aye-aye, Captain." She saluted him as she picked up her portfolio and opened the office door just as Wilma started in. "And ... Josh?" She tried to put a certain sexy huskiness into her voice for Wilma's benefit. "I'm really looking forward to our evening together." With delight she saw the color that rose to his cheeks as Wilma took her place in the chair opposite him.

# Five

They met in the library. Marlo had changed into a dress she hoped would be appropriate both for meeting the famous J. P. Carrington and for enticing that look of longing from Josh' eyes that she'd seen more than once. She'd chosen a midcalf length dress of deep blue jersey. The neckline was scooped, but not so daringly that anyone could accuse her of impropriety, and she accented the outfit with a chunky gold and brass necklace she'd discovered at a local Milwaukee art gallery. Black calf pumps with two-inch heels and hosiery that picked up a hint of the color of the dress completed the outfit.

J. P. Carrington, wearing pants, a shirt, tie and tweed sport jacket, was seated in his wheelchair next to the fire. The fire brought out the highlights in his full head of white hair, and his eyes were bright and penetratingly direct. Marlo was somewhat relieved to see Sally in attendance for this meeting, because Josh seemed more nervous than Marlo herself. So much for inspiring confidence in him, she thought ruefully.

Sally, dressed in a gray suit, was genuinely glad to see her and floated across the room on ridiculously high heels to take

Marlo's clammy hands in her own and led her closer to the fire. "I promise you that despite appearances to the contrary, neither of them bites," she whispered, glancing from her son to the patriarch in the wheelchair. "J.P., this is Marlo Fletcher."

"Mr. Carrington." Marlo offered her hand, and he took it firmly, his eyes never wavering from their close inspection of her, as if there were some test to be passed in the shaking of hands.

"Miss Fletcher," he acknowledged her, and waited.

"What can I get you to drink, Marlo?" Sally, playing the hostess, bustled back to the bar.

"Just some club soda, please," Marlo answered, hoping that it would succeed in calming her jumpy stomach.

"J.P.? Joshua?" Sally solicited their orders while filling a glass with ice and soda for Marlo.

"For heaven's sake, Sally, this is a business meeting, not afternoon cocktails," J.P. muttered.

"Brandy then, J.P.?" Sally replied sweetly as she handed Marlo her soda. "Sit down, Marlo. Even business meetings don't have to be so starchy. People tend to accomplish so much more when they're relaxed and enjoying the work. Don't you agree, Joshua?"

"Mother." He was smiling at her, but it was a firm warning. "Could we get on with this? Marlo has a great deal of ground to cover." He opened Marlo's portfolio, removed the files and sketches and spread them over the leather-topped game table. "Grandfather, could you come over here? I think it will be easier to discuss what Patrick and Marlo have planned."

J.P. unlocked the brakes on his chair and rolled it to within inches of where Marlo sat. "Miss Fletcher," he said, indicating with his hand that he was waiting for her to precede him to the table. "You understand that these days my grandson makes the decisions concerning Carrington's. I've been inactive in the business for some time now. His bringing you here today is purely a courtesy, I assure you."

Marlo nodded and then moved quickly into her presentation. Her nervousness vanished as she warmed to her subject, and she recorded the gleam of interest in the older man's eyes as he scrutinized each sketch and budget sheet. Despite what he'd told her, she knew he could veto any aspect of the campaign with a mere shake of his head. She also knew it was important to Joshua that his grandfather approve of what he was doing to revitalize the store. Meeting those intelligent if aging gray eyes became her greatest challenge, and before she'd finished presenting the plans for opening night, she found herself enjoying J.P.'s scrutiny.

"Still, the success of the plan depends on much more than one week of special events and the gala," she said, moving smoothly into her presentation of the idea to retrain the staff. "Sally, that's a lovely suit you're wearing. Do you mind standing for a minute and helping me with the next part?"

With a smile of delight, Sally Carrington rose and took her place next to Marlo, who held the attention of everyone present. "From what I've been able to gather from the various departments, eighty-five percent of the purchases at Carrington's are made by women—even purchases in the men's departments. Assume that Sally is a typical Carrington shopper. She needs a suit for meetings and business appointments. But neither a man nor a woman simply purchases a suit. The suit needs to be accessorized to make it belong uniquely to that customer. Chances are there'll be six to eight of the same suits on the rack when our customer comes in. Also, the suit is expensive. If Sally's on a budget, she may forgo the suit even though it's well made and will last her through a number of seasons. She may decide that it would be better to spread her money around on cheaper items so that she can have more. The salesperson's responsibility is to show Sally that by adding the right accessories, this suit can become the starting point around which an entire wardrobe is built. Let me show you."

For the next several minutes she demonstrated the variety of looks Sally might create from her simple gray silk suit. Marlo was excited by the spark of interest that flared in the senior Carrington's eyes as she completed the display. He was ready for the punch line. "The problem with this scenario is twofold. One, rarely is a salesperson properly trained to offer so many ideas to a customer in such a short time, and two, the pieces necessary to sell those ideas may be located in departments that are two or three floors away."

Josh leaned eagerly toward his grandfather. "You see, J.P., by making the staff walking models of our ability in fashion coordination and by moving departments in such a way that accessories wind up next to basic pieces, we can offer each customer the same kind of personalized service you just saw here today."

"I see," Sally put in. "What you are proposing is that if I came in next week to pick up something for Florida, I would find the sundress and with it the sandals and the belt and the purse?"

"Not only that," Marlo added. "Eventually each salesperson would be so well trained that a schoolteacher leaving for a week in New York over spring break would be able to walk into Carrington's and say to the salesperson, 'I have X dollars to spend and I need these pieces to fill out my wardrobe.' The salesperson could then present a selection of items in the proper price range." She paused.

"Well, I just love the whole idea," Sally said as she pulled the revised floor plans toward her to study them more carefully. "It takes the hassle out of trying to do everything for yourself. I can't stand it when I have to run from store to store looking for just the right top or shoes. What you're doing here is putting the fun back into shopping."

Joshua sat back in his chair and lavished a smile of pride on Marlo. Flushed with success, she turned her full attention once again to J.P. He was studying the figures on the proposed budget sheets with a decided frown, and there was no enthusiasm coming from him.

"Joshua, would it offend you if Miss Fletcher and I spent a few moments alone? I have some questions about all this."

Joshua was on guard at once, but Sally spoke before he could say anything. "How lovely. It's high time the two of you got to know each other better. Come along, Joshua. You wanted me to remind you to call for reservations. This is perfect timing. You'll be finished with Marlo by seven, won't you, J.P.?" Sally smiled and patted Marlo's hand as she and Josh left, sliding the twin oak doors closed behind them.

For a full minute there was no sound in the room other than the occasional crackle of the fire and the shuffling of papers by J.P.

"Miss Fletcher," he said finally, "let's move back to the fire." Again he indicated that she was to go first. "Would you like something more to drink?"

"No, thank you," Marlo answered, then forced herself to fold her hands serenely in her lap. Her normal reaction would have been to try to anticipate his questions and doubts, but something told her that with this man she should simply wait.

"You've done some very good work here. How much of the history of the Carrington firm have you heard?"

Marlo briefly recounted those parts she'd gathered from Josh and Patrick and other employees. J.P. listened, nodding from time to time until she came to the years when the store had operated under Josh's father. At the mention of his son, J.P. became restless and somewhat agitated, his outward calm cracking around the edges. She tried to give her remarks about that time a diplomatic tone, but there was little anyone could have done to sugarcoat the facts. "From what I can understand," she finished, "at the time of the second Mr. Carrington's accident, the store was in deep financial trouble, and you, sir, were unable to take back the reins because of your health. I believe it was at that point that Joshua became your designated successor."

"And he was far too young," the older man said almost to himself as if continuing her narration. "Just barely out of that fancy Eastern business school, just beginning to really learn the ropes. I never finished high school. Did you know that, Miss Fletcher?"

She shook her head but said nothing.

"No, my education was on the job. I was a good student, and when hard times came, Carrington's maintained its status. As a matter of fact, it flourished."

"And it will again," Marlo said, bringing him back to the present.

"Will it?" He stared at her quietly, daring her to back up her statement. "My son attended those same fancy schools he sent my grandson to, and look where he took the store."

"As I understand it, sir," Marlo replied quietly, "your son's interests were in areas that had little to do with retailing. Surely you can see that your grandson is as addicted to the business as you once were. He thrives on the challenge of it, and he's determined to prove to himself and to you that he can turn it around."

"And you're going to help him?" He didn't wait for an answer. "Just what is your interest in my grandson, Miss Fletcher? You come from another part of the country, from another profession, and yet here you are, living in this house and taking a major role in both the business and my grandson's life."

For the first time since she'd been left alone with J.P., Marlo smiled openly. "Mr. Carrington, your grandson and I are about to go out for dinner—probably to continue discussing the spring campaign, if I know him at all. I would hardly qualify that as 'taking a major role' in your grandson's life. As for living here—"

"I know that was Sally's idea. The woman is a born meddler and matchmaker. If she thought she could find someone who could stand me, she'd have married me off again." Marlo didn't miss the fondness that edged his voice or the softening of his features when he talked of his daughter-in-law. "But you haven't answered my question."

"Originally I came here because of my friendship with Patrick Dean. He was in a bind. I needed the money, and he offered me a temporary solution to both our problems. Quite frankly, I liked the idea of an opportunity to prove to myself that my designs could work, could solve a problem, could help a project in another arena. And now that I'm here, I'm very much enjoying the work and the people. I had no idea that retailing had so much in common with the theater, but in some ways it *is* theater, isn't it?" She didn't wait for an answer. "I'm also enjoying your city. We New Yorkers tend to live in a vacuum, you know. We can be terrible snobs when it comes to the hinterlands, I'm afraid."

She was rewarded with a smile, and she could see that she was gaining ground. "You have some very interesting ideas," he commented, casting a glance back at the game table, which was still covered by her files and sketches. "Expensive, but interesting. I suppose you are aware that in the sixties, your own Bloomingdale's put into effect a similar boutique concept, and it was widely copied across the country."

"Yes. But what Patrick and I propose to do will go beyond that. We plan to build our concept around your founding principles of selling top-quality merchandise in innovative surroundings by informed sales personnel. The root of the idea is quality *plus* service."

"You're done your homework, Miss Fletcher. I like that." He leaned back in his chair and studied her for a moment. "I'm sure that Sally or Josh has told you my feelings about the family fraternizing with the hired help."

Marlo smiled at the archaic expression and nodded.

"I have good reason for that, young lady. When a man and woman work closely together, it's easy to misread the feelings that are exchanged. The rush of adrenaline that comes with a hurdle overcome, the pride of accomplishing a goal through good teamwork, can be mistaken for something more. My son mistook his feelings for a co-worker for something more, Miss Fletcher, and that nearly spelled disaster for him and Sally and for Carrington's. Milwaukee is in many ways a small town, and the people don't easily tolerate scandal."

She decided to remain silent, though she was bursting to tell him that Joshua's seeing her was hardly the same thing as a married man having an affair with an employee. For that matter, after what had happened in her apartment the night before, it hardly seemed likely that Josh would lose his head in the heat of passion.

"My grandson is too good in some ways, Miss Fletcher. He works too hard at making dreams come true for old men, for one thing. Does it surprise you that I recognize that he's doing all this for me?" Marlo murmured a no, and he continued. "But it does surprise you that I would allow him to continue to seek my approval when in fact he already has it?"

She nodded.

"Joshua has had a difficult life in spite of all of this." He waved a hand to indicate their luxurious surroundings. "Perhaps because of all of this. His father was not much of a par-

ent to the boy. I think that was because my son never saw
himself as adult enough to have fathered a child. He was a delightful, spoiled man for most of his life, and I think I demanded too much of him—more than he could give. By the
time I realized that, it was too late.''

"I think Joshua may be trying to make up for his father's
deficiencies,'' Marlo ventured, though she was loath to stop the
stream of information the older man was offering her.

"Even as a small boy, Joshua took the role of duty over
pleasure. There isn't the slightest doubt in my mind that he'll
succeed in making Carrington's a resounding success.''

"Then why don't you tell him that?'' Marlo was so surprised she forgot herself for the moment.

"I have my reasons. In the meantime, I suspect that you're
very good for him, and in spite of my reservations, I hope that
you enjoy your dinner. As for your business acumen, time will
tell if you can translate those ideas into action as successfully
as you transmit them to paper.'' He offered her his hand, and
there was a marked difference from their introductory handshake. This time, although the element of challenge remained,
the gesture was tempered with respect and admiration.


"How did it go with J.P.?'' Josh asked after they were seated
in the plush surroundings of the restaurant.

"Fine,'' she answered. "He has some obvious reservations
about my ability to pull this off in time, but then that's rea-
sonable.''

The waiter interrupted them to take their order. Josh frowned
and deferred to Marlo, who seemed surprisingly relaxed and
calm after her time alone with his grandfather.

"What did you think?'' she asked, buttering a slice of bread
after the waiter had left.

"I wasn't there,'' he replied tersely.

"Of course you were. It was better having you there during
the presentation than Patrick. I couldn't have had a more avid
supporter—unless, of course, you count Sally.''

That brought relaxation to his features and a smile. "She's
really taken with you, you know.''

"Your mom is a pushover. Your grandfather is another story. But I thought it went very well, didn't you?"

He almost choked on his soup, and then composed himself and studied her closely. "Okay, what exactly happened when the two of you were alone?"

Marlo shrugged. "Not much. He ran down the history of the store for me. He seemed to like our ideas, but he made it clear the final decision rests with you." That elicited a grunt from Josh. "Is that supposed to mean something?"

"Don't be fooled, Marlo. My grandfather founded this business. He watches over every detail of it, especially since..." He stopped in midsentence, apparently recalling his rule not to discuss family business with outsiders.

"Especially since he once entrusted the business to your father and that didn't work out so well? We talked about that." She was beginning to be very glad that she'd decided not to offer him a detailed description of her conversation with J.P. She found it fun to drop these little surprises when he least expected them.

"He discussed my father with you?"

"Only in the context of the history of the store. We also talked about you—in the context of the history of the store, of course." She grinned wickedly at him, and he smiled back.

"You're enjoying this, aren't you?"

For several moments they were silent while the waiter served their dinner and the wine. When conversation resumed, Josh immediately returned to the subject of the store, but Marlo stopped him.

"Josh, no offense, but I've been eating, sleeping, and breathing Carrington's since Friday. Couldn't we just talk without having it relate to business?"

"Okay." He cut into his steak and waited.

Marlo sighed and plunged in. "Well, tell me about you."

"What do you want to know?"

"Is there a reason why a man of your age still lives at home?" she blurted out before she had time to think.

He laughed long and loud. "Are you concerned that a man of my advanced years must be a momma's boy because he still lives with her?"

She blushed furiously, uncomfortable with her boldness. It was certainly none of her business why he lived at home.

"I had my own place for a while. But when my grandfather became ill and my parents were away so much, I decided someone should be in the house. Has Mom given you the grand tour?"

"With the exception of your rooms," she answered quietly. She was beginning to wish she'd never started this conversation. Suddenly the subject of business seemed much safer.

"Then you know the house was designed to accommodate more than one family. My grandparents planned it that way. They wanted their children to have all the comforts of home once they married. It really is very nice and extremely private."

"So you moved back to care for your grandfather?"

He chuckled. "I told myself that was it. The truth was I hated the apartment I had. It was one of those high-rise complexes. A lot of single professional people. It was damned lonely there."

"I know," she said, recalling her own apartment in New York. The idea that one would get to know neighbors and form friendships was more often than not a myth.

"Do you like sports?"

He nodded. "Basketball, tennis, football, baseball." He started to grin. "Actually, there doesn't seem to be a sport I don't like."

"We'll start with basketball. Do you play?"

"When there's time, and then the store—whoops. Let me rephrase that. We—uh—have some season tickets for the Bucks. How's that for staying off business?"

"You're catching on." She smiled. "Don't the Bucks play tonight? Against the Knicks, as I recall."

"How did you know that?"

"There are other sports fans than just you, Mr. Carrington. Why didn't you go to the game?"

"I wanted to take you out for dinner."

"Why?" She put her fork down and watched him, her eyes daring him to be less than honest in his answer. "Because you liked my presentation?"

"Oh, I like your presentation all right," he commented. He made it clear with a look that he meant the way the blue jersey hugged her body, not the way she planned to renovate the store. "Why did you accept?" He suddenly felt shy, and he admitted her answer meant a great deal to him.

"Because I wanted to," she answered simply, and then added unnecessarily, "because I wanted to be with you somewhere other than Carrington's."

"That's becoming a problem for me as well."

At that she leaned forward and grasped his hand. "Why does it have to be a problem, Josh? We like each other. Why does everything have to be carried out as if we were robots programmed to do our jobs without any opportunity for friendship or attraction to develop?"

He focused on her smaller hand covering his large one but made no move to break contact. "I told you. I have to concern myself with the business right now. We're so close to success, Marlo. I can't allow myself to become distracted at this stage."

"Why? Because your grandfather would be disappointed or because you'd be proven to be like your father, a man with no head for business? Your grandfather admires you very much, Josh. He told me—" She stopped herself in midsentence. Josh needed to learn of his grandfather's approval on his own, not to have it delivered through her.

"What did he tell you?"

"He told me you work too hard," she said. "And he's right. Burying yourself in your work, no matter how noble the cause, is no way to live. Trying to live your life to please another person is like being in prison. People respect you for just being who you are, and they don't really care whether or not you're human and make some mistakes along the way."

"I'm doing what I want," he insisted a bit defensively.

"Not everything," she challenged. "For example, wouldn't you like to go to that ball game?"

"Well, of course, but there'll be other games."

"And you'll find one excuse after another to not be there. When are you going to understand that it's possible to have more than one thing at a time in life, Josh? You don't have to be so cautious all the time." She pulled her hand free and sat back with a sigh of exasperation.

"Okay," he said softly, "tonight you've earned the right to take over. I've been teaching you retailing. Tonight you show me what you consider to be reality." He was smiling broadly at her.

"No backing out? No turning into a pumpkin at midnight?" He held up his hand in promise. "Okay—" she grinned "—you're on. First, finish your dinner, and then let's get out of here. It's a lovely place but a bit stuffy for the evening I have in mind."

They finished their meal with gusto, and then Josh paid the check. Outside Marlo hailed a cab. "What about my car?" Josh asked.

"Takes too long to park it. Leave it here, and we'll walk back for it later. I hope you brought the tickets for the game."

"I have them—only because I meant to give them to Patrick, though. But Marlo, the first half will be nearly over by the time we get there."

"So? Unless you play by different rules out here in the boondocks, basketball has two halves, and things aren't decided until the final buzzer. Five bucks say the Knicks beat your guys."

"Are you serious? The Knicks can't beat us on the home court. We're contenders for the championship this year, you know."

"Ha! The championship is still months away, mister, and everybody's a contender—it's a new season. So put your money where your mouth is, Carrington."

The game was well into the second quarter when they arrived. For the next two hours they cheered their respective teams, Marlo taking a lot of good-natured heat from surrounding Bucks fans as she cheered for her Knicks. Although she appeared to be engrossed in the game, her attention was really on the man beside her. She was delighted to see him let go of some tension and stress by cheering for his team or loudly chastising the referees for what he insisted were totally unfair calls.

Marlo found herself seeking excuses to touch him—when the game went into overtime, when a player was on the floor with an unknown injury, when the Knicks' center stunned the crowd with a fantastic dunk shot. She would alternately pound his shoulder or grip his strong forearm, and when the seconds ticked down to zero and the Knicks had the ball and an opportunity to score the final basket, she gripped his hand tightly as the players raced from one end of the court to the other. Just as the clock went from one second to zero, the ball was hurled into the air, and bounced off the rim and the Milwaukee crowd cheered lustily. Josh pulled Marlo hard against his side and hugged her, raising a triumphant fist in the air.

After the heat of the arena, the night air felt cold and crisp and refreshing, and the walk back to the car was exhilarating. They discussed the game, and Josh demanded payment of the bet. Defiantly Marlo reached into her purse for her wallet, but Josh closed his hand over hers.

"What are you doing?" he asked in a serious tone, but there was the hint of a gleam in his eye as they stood under a street lamp waiting for the light to change.

"I'm getting your five dollars," she replied huffily.

"Nope. *You* bet five dollars—that's what you wanted from me. We never discussed what I wanted from you if *I* won."

"What do you want?" she asked, noting that for such a cold night it was becoming increasingly warm on this particular corner.

"I want..." He leaned closer, and Marlo waited breathlessly for his kiss. "I want you..." He paused for the barest second before continuing. "I want you to buy me the biggest hot fudge sundae we can find." And then he stepped away and started across the street.

Marlo had been so ready for the taste of his lips on hers that she'd actually closed her eyes. In the next minute she opened them to find him halfway across the now deserted street. "Carrington, you're in big trouble," she shouted as she charged across the street after him.

He turned to meet her and he was laughing. "Come here," he called softly, opening his arms to her. "Just to show you what a good winner I am," he said, then lowered his head to kiss her. There was no delicacy, no foreplay of nibbles or teasing. One minute they were playful—the next he held her in a viselike grip and was ravaging every corner of her surprised mouth.

Inching her arms from his strong hold, she circled them around his neck and pulled his head closer, answering his explorations with forays of her own. He moved his hands over her back and hips and around her waist, and she was aware that every possible inch of their bodies was in contact. It was frustrating, for her bulky coat prevented the kind of touch he obviously wanted.

"Damned winter weather," he muttered against her hair when he pulled away to catch some sanity from the cold night air, willing himself to regain control.

No, she wanted to protest when she felt him withdraw, don't let go of what we have.

Hoping to recapture the spirit of the evening, she ventured, "How about that sundae?"

"Ice cream on a night like this?" He smiled down at her. "Now you've got to admit that isn't what your normal conservative Midwesterner would suggest."

"See what progress you've made already," she answered as she pushed some of the hair away from his forehead. "I'm really a terrific teacher, aren't I?"

"I'll just bet," he said, but the smile had been replaced by a slight furrowing of his thick brows. He took a deep breath and moved her a safe distance away before taking her hand in a purely friendly motion as they continued toward the car. "Ice cream it is. Kopp's, I think."

They drove north into the suburbs and stopped at a frozen-custard stand on a busy strip lined with every imaginable franchise. There was no place to sit except on the edge of the stone borders that framed lush green plants. Josh asked Marlo what she liked, and she told him to surprise her. He returned with a gooey confection that looked as if it were meant for several people rather than just one small woman.

"Cashew Creation," he announced as he presented her with the overflowing dish.

"Joshua, there has to be a quart of custard in this thing, not to mention half a pound of nuts and a pint of topping. I can't eat this."

"Where's your adventure now, Ms. Fletcher? Don't New Yorkers eat fattening foods?"

"New Yorkers *invented* fattening foods, but this..." She took her first bite of the huge sundae. "This," she continued between bites, "is fabulous." And with that she was silent for several minutes as she wolfed it down.

"No one's going to take it away from you, Marlo," Josh said with a smile as he savored his own sundae.

"That's not the problem. If I don't eat at this pace, I'll still be here in the morning trying to finish." She stopped to catch her breath and grinned at him.

"This has been fun," Josh said, sounding a little surprised at the admission.

"Progress, at last," she said softly. They ate in silence for a few minutes, people-watching as they sat close to each other and observed the other patrons. "See that guy?" Marlo nodded to a rumpled, sleepy man at the counter. "His wife is pregnant and has just gotten the pickles-and-ice-cream munchies."

"What about that woman?" Josh asked, catching on at once.

"She's on her way home to curl up alone with a good romance novel and nine thousand calories."

"That's a pretty sad story," Josh said.

"I don't know. There are times when a person needs that kind of escapism. It's only sad when a person has no choice. Sometimes I like being alone without having to think about anyone else."

"Really?" Josh seemed to turn his full attention to his sundae.

"That doesn't mean I want to be alone all the time, you understand, or even most of the time."

"What happens when you don't want to go to bed alone?" He still hadn't looked directly at her, so intent was he on scraping the last drop of fudge from the bottom of his cup.

"Josh Carrington, that's a very direct question coming from someone as reticent as you!" She laughed, then took his cup and her own and tossed them into the wastebasket. "To answer your question, Josh, it's hardly as simple as I make it sound. It means I make a decision to work at a relationship because I'm interested to see where it might lead."

"Sounds pretty clinical," he said as he helped her into his car.

"Not a bit. I'm working very hard at this relationship. Does it feel clinical?" She ran one finger lightly along his thigh and felt the car pull sharply to one side.

"Cut that out," he muttered, "before I run off the road."

When they were in the garage below her apartment, he switched off the motor and then turned to look at her, playing with her hair, stroking her cheek. "You have the most incredible skin," he whispered, and leaned closer to plant kisses along the curve of her chin.

"Would you like to come inside?" Her voice sounded far away, drowned out by the roar of need that raced through her head and body.

"Of course I want to come in with you. You're aware by now that the idea that I could actually concentrate on business without thinking of you was pure folly," he said gruffly, pulling her hard against his chest. He took her lips under his in a fierce kiss that left no doubt of his desire.

Marlo thoroughly enjoyed the multiple sensations that surrounded her in that moment: the rush of cold air, followed immediately by the warmth of Josh's hand when he opened her heavy coat to explore the outline of her breasts; the mixture of the scent of the leather interior of the car with the woolly roughness of his jacket against her face; the taste of his tongue.

"You taste of chocolate," she laughed, using her tongue to outline the shape of his mouth when they briefly pulled apart.

"This way, at least, it has no calories," he whispered, and pulled her back into his arms for another long, searching kiss.

"Josh?" She pushed gently against his chest as she felt him searching for closer contact to her skin. "Wouldn't this be easier and more comfortable inside?" But her hands seemed to

have a mind of their own as they sought to memorize the shap
of him beneath his suit and topcoat.

He groaned and set her away from him, pulling her co
closed to cover her. "It would be. But not tonight. We're bo
too tired and have too many other things waiting to be take
care of. When we make love, I want it to be slowly and tho
oughly done. I don't want to have to stop and punch a clock

"You're the boss," she reminded him. "You don't have
punch clocks."

"Bosses punch mental clocks," he said firmly as he bu
toned her coat up to her neck. "And this boss needs his be
designer fresh and ready to take action on those dynamic d
signs first thing in the morning."

"Okay, boss, but I just want you to know we aren't going
lose ground because of this."

"I'll buy that," he said, and kissed her lightly on the lip
Then he started to comb his fingers through his hair.

"Stop that," Marlo said, messing up his hair again. "Yo
aren't the executive now, Josh. You've been kissing a woma
It isn't necessary to look as if you just stepped out of the pag
of *GQ*." There was a sharpness to her tone that sounded like
mixture of anger and perhaps a little fear.

"Marlo, please understand that it's important that we ke
this separate from our relationship at the store."

"I don't understand that at all, Josh. We're human bein
with multifaceted lives. I've never understood cataloging n
life into neat little compartments. I'm not going to embarra
you at the store, but neither can I forget during the hours
nine to five what we have between us." She drew away fro
him to open the door.

He reached over and pulled her back. "I'm not asking yo
to do that," he insisted.

"Aren't you, Josh?" she said wearily. "Does that mean I ca
talk openly about our dinner tonight and the game and t
sundae? About our 'date,' Josh? Because whether you like it
not, that's what it was. From the minute we left this house,
wasn't business, and we both knew it. Are you ready for Pa
rick's ribbing for breaking one of your own unwritten rules?

don't think so." She saw by the expression on his face that he was playing the scenario through his mind, and she knew she was right. "That's what I thought. Good night, Joshua. I'll see you at work."

# Six

———

By the time Josh made it to the store the following day, it was nearly noon. A heavy schedule of committee and financial meetings had kept him busy through the morning, and he had to admit he'd stalled a bit, not wanting to run into Marlo so soon after their disagreement. He needed time to mull over their problem of mutual attraction and working together. Not that he hadn't spent a great deal of time mulling it over already. He hadn't slept much the night before.

On top of that, he'd gotten some bad news that morning that would affect both him and Marlo on several levels. Patrick had called to say that he'd hurt his back lifting some boxes. Patrick's back had been a problem of his since college, and Josh had seen his friend in such pain that it made him wince to think of it. This time Patrick had really done it. According to the doctor, he was to remain in bed for at least two weeks. There was even some discussion of surgery to remove the offending disk.

"I'll get back as soon as I can, Josh," Patrick had promised that morning when Josh stopped by to see if there was any thing he could do for him. "Damn. I hate that this had to happen now."

They'd agreed that Josh would keep him informed of the progress at the store and let Patrick help by making calls and dictating ad copy from his bed.

As Josh strode up the avenue now, he caught a glimpse of movement in one of the front windows. What better way to judge Marlo's mood than with a plate of glass between them? He walked over to the window and watched her work, waiting for her to become aware of him. She was doing a display of glassware, carefully pyramiding the crystal on levels of deep green velvet. As usual, there was a flair in her work; the display was nothing ordinary, for peeking out from the formal green velvet were bunches of silk daisies tied with multicolored ribbons.

The unexpected touch of whimsy made Josh smile. In the sharp February wind roaring up the avenue straight off the lake, he was thinking of picnics in the park with his parents and grandparents. Those had been special times—times before his father and grandfather had knocked heads over business. The memories made him temporarily forget that he'd come to see Marlo and gauge her mood from the safe distance of the street.

A tapping brought him back to the reality of the winter afternoon. Marlo was leaning against the other side of the glass, watching him. She gave him a questioning smile and a slight salute. Apparently she'd been watching him for several seconds. Josh straightened, returned her salutation with a thumbs-up sign toward the display, turned up the collar of his overcoat and walked briskly past and into the store. He stopped by the window where she was working and told her about Patrick. While she went off to call her friend, Josh went to his office to organize a staff meeting and assign Patrick some help.

By late that afternoon everything was under control. With the staff he'd been able to work out a plan for keeping Patrick involved as much as possible and at the same time cover what he'd be unable to handle. The one thing Josh knew he would be taking over personally was the time that Patrick would have spent with Marlo working toward the deadline of the spring gala. He told himself that he couldn't entrust such an impor-

tant component of the plan to anyone other than Patrick and
that without Patrick, he'd just have to work with her himself.

As if on cue, Marlo came into his office. "Got a minute,
boss?"

"Sure, what's up?"

"Well, Patrick and I have been working on the opening-night
gala by phone most of the day, and we have an interesting idea
for our charge customers. Got time now?"

"Of course." Josh tried to sound hearty. Marlo was stun-
ning in a red jump suit with padded shoulders, her slender waist
wrapped in a wide leather belt.

"It came to our attention that the week of the opening coin-
cides with your grandfather's eightieth birthday. We thought
it would really kick things off if we sponsored the Roaring
Twenties party for our 'preferred customers' in honor of J.P.
as the founder of the store."

"It is a good idea," he began slowly.

"But . . . ?" Marlo prompted him.

"Marlo, they're all wonderful ideas—the retraining of the
staff, the makeovers, the remodeling and the reorganiza-
tion . . ."

"But—let me guess—they're all expensive ideas, right?"

"Exactly." Josh loosened the knot on his tie and opened the
top button of his shirt. Marlo was beginning to notice that
lately, more often than not, he wasn't always the perfect show-
case for his own fashion image. "We're talking thousands of
dollars just for this party," he said. "This morning I presented your other ideas to our accountants and legal staff. They
thought I'd lost my mind to authorize so many drastic changes
at once. They wanted to know what J.P. thought of so many
major moves. . . ."

His words hung in the air between them, and Marlo suspected he was nursing a wounded pride. She began to understand that his zeal to revitalize the business had as much to do
with proving himself to the community on his own merits as it
did with honoring his grandfather.

"But it's the perfect kickoff," Marlo said as she concen-
trated on wearing a path in the carpeting.

Suddenly Josh pounded his desk and his face was split by a huge grin. "I've got it! J.P.'s favorite charity is the MACC Fund—Midwest Athletes against Childhood Cancer. What if we throw this bash for J.P. but we charge people to come?"

"Josh," Marlo reminded him gently, "I thought you were having trouble getting people to come into the store for free. How in the world are we going to make them pay for the privilege?"

"We can charge them because all of the proceeds after expenses will go the MACC Fund in honor of J.P.'s eightieth birthday. Everyone dresses up. We have an orchestra, dancing, appetizers, desserts, cocktails—we could even serve bathtub gin in the lingerie area."

Marlo was spellbound by Josh's enthusiasm. "It's great!" she marveled. "And we could have dance contests and prizes for the best twenties costume."

"We could even invite the athletes who are in town as guests of honor—you know how people love meeting their sports heroes!" Josh was pacing with excitement now as the plans came together.

"Better yet, get the athletes to act as celebrity waiters and their tips go into the pot for the MACC Fund," Marlo added.

"Not bad." Josh pondered the idea. "And we could have the staff all dressed up and helping out with security. It's just great, isn't it?" The little boy Marlo had seen in the photographs was back and full of anticipation. "And I think the two of us are just the ones to pull this off." He was grinning from ear to ear. Marlo's heart flip-flopped, and her voice went on strike.

"But..." Josh held up a warning finger, his professional sternness back in place.

"Always with the buts," Marlo groaned.

"But," Josh continued firmly, "we have to discuss the other ideas you and Patrick have dreamed up. The accountants tell me these projects will have to be accomplished over a longer period of time or we'll be bankrupt before we even make it to the gala."

"That's okay," Marlo said, and he looked at her with surprise. "Well, you hardly want to put all your best shots into one week. What on earth would you do for an encore? No, it's better to leave them wanting more and then be able to deliver in the coming months."

"Perhaps," Joshua said as he looked back at the ledger sheets on his desk. "For now, let's concentrate on the party—it must pay for itself. If we can set that up, then you have clearance to rearrange the store. Just be sure we don't have to apologize for ladders and paint buckets on the night of the party. If you start it, then plan on having it finished by the party, understood?"

"And after that we can move into the makeovers and seminars," Marlo continued.

"We'll see about that part of it after we get past this first step," Joshua said, and stood to indicate that as far as he was concerned the meeting was over.

"Wait a minute. What's changed, Josh? Yesterday you knew the figures, but you were all for the entire package. I can't believe that the meeting with the bankers has set you back so much."

"We have to be practical, Marlo. You may not be with us for the time it'll take to put all your plans into action. And while I'm certainly enthusiastic about all the ideas you and Patrick have presented, I just think it's time that a cooler head prevailed. We've worked five long years to get where we are, and I just don't want us to get in over our heads now that we've come so close. What if Patrick has to have surgery? You'll be back in New York. Who knows how long he'd be in the hospital and then be away for recovery?"

"Of course, you're right," Marlo said, hoping to hide the hurt she felt at his seeming doubts about her ability to deliver what she'd promised. "I realize I'm an unknown quantity here—a novice at retailing and a temporary employee to boot. Drawing the picture is one thing, but it's time to see if I can deliver the goods. Right, Josh?"

"All I'm asking is that we take this one step at a time. Start with the party. If you can come up with the figures on that to show that it will pay for itself, then go ahead with moving things around in the store. We're running out of time, Marlo. The hour for coming up with the ideas has just passed, and now we need some concrete results, okay?"

He saw her flinch at his words and realized for the first time that he was capable of causing her pain. He came around his large desk and sat in the chair next to hers, so close that their knees almost touched.

"I'm sorry, Marlo. I was out of line. I didn't mean to imply that you couldn't execute these wonderful plans you seem to brim over with. I just need for you to understand that I have learned caution the hard way. Five years ago, everything seemed so simple. Patrick and I would simply restore Carrington's original quality and the customers would return in force. But we've had to fight for every inch of headway. This—" he indicated the large calendar before them "—has been repeatedly revised, with the deadline set back several times."

"Look, Josh." She reached over and patted the back of his hand in a gesture of friendship and understanding. "This is your life—not some game. You're absolutely right to be concerned about me. I'm here on loan, so to speak. In a month or so, when the gala is history and George is back, he'll have a thousand other ideas and I'll be on my way back to the theater and New York. Please, don't ever apologize to me for taking care of your own career."

"I'm not sure that I like that—the idea that you're already planning to go away. I guess I thought we could tempt you to stay on through the summer at least." He was playing with her fingers and not looking at her.

Marlo pulled her hand away and stood up. "Let's get one thing straight, Josh," she said softly. "You set some rules last night that I intend to try to live up to—separation of business and pleasure. When you say things like that and touch me like that, you're bending the rules. Well, let me tell you that it's going to be hard enough to rein in my natural attraction to you without you throwing me curves like those. Let's just stick to business, okay?"

"Marlo," he said, moving toward her.

"I've got a lot of work to do," she said nervously, backing toward the door. "If there isn't anything else—"

"We're not finished with this, Marlo Fletcher," he said warningly as she stood with her back to him, her hand on the doorknob.

She turned then and her eyes flashed. "Perhaps not, Joshua, but let me tell you this. For someone who doesn't like playing games, you're awfully good at them. You also have a tendency to make up the rules as it suits your whim, and you're going to have a hard time getting me to play under those conditions. See you at the meeting tomorrow. Good night."

"Carrington, you're an idiot," Joshua muttered to himself as the door closed softly but firmly behind her.

Within the week, Marlo and Patrick convinced Josh that the party would definitely make money for the charity. Marlo and Josh began working together to coordinate the efforts to reorganize the store and have it ready in time for the gala. Night after night they stayed late with the carpentry crew and, on paper, changed merchandise from one area of the store to another. The actual construction would be done in the workshop, and then the store would close for three days before the party while the entire staff worked to put everything in place.

"I think we're almost there," Marlo announced cheerfully one Friday night as they sat in Josh's office, eating pizza. "In just three weeks we'll be giving the party of the year. I feel like celebrating."

"I thought this was celebrating," Josh joked. "For once, the pizza's still hot."

Over the past week they'd been together more than they'd been apart, usually buffered by other staff members but more than once alone. Those times had been unbearably tense for both of them. Marlo had remained resolute in her determination to stick to business, but her need for him to hold her had almost driven her crazy. She was irritable, tired of putting up a cheery front.

Josh sat back and looked at her over his soft drink. "This isn't working, Marlo."

"I know," she answered quietly, not pretending for one second that she didn't know what he was talking about. She wasn't the type to be coy, especially when the subject was such a serious one.

"I can't work with you day in and night out and hold my feelings in check," Josh said. "I can't lie there in that huge house—especially now that Mom and J.P. are in Florida—and not think about what you might be doing, how you're sleeping, what you're sleeping in."

She smiled at that. "Those are some pretty racy thoughts for the president of a major department store, Mr. Carrington."

He grinned sheepishly at her. "That's nothing! I censored the real thing."

"I'd rather hear the real thing," she almost whispered.

"I'm not sure either of us could handle that," he replied gruffly, and busied himself gathering the remains of their dinner and disposing of the cartons and cups. "Can I take you home?" he asked. When she nodded, he led the way from his office to hers, waiting while she put her ever-present sketches and papers into her portfolio.

Marlo and Josh were quiet on the ride home.

The massive house was completely dark except for one light in the front hallway. Until the day before the party, Josh was there alone.

"Looks pretty spooky with the moon behind it like that, doesn't it?" Marlo tried to keep her tone light. The emotions that had been shadowing her and Josh all night were threatening to take solid form, but she knew he'd expect her to keep their bargain.

"If you're not totally exhausted," Josh said as he opened the car door and offered her his hand, "how about coming in for a brandy?"

She started to giggle and then gave a full laugh. "Joshua Carrington, you don't even like brandy."

"I know," he said with a laugh. "I'm not at all good at this—trying to be romantic and sophisticated. I should take lessons from Patrick."

"Just say what you mean," Marlo challenged him as she accepted his hand and deliberately stepped close to him out of the car.

"What I mean is I want you to come in with me because I don't want to let you go, because if I don't take you in my arms and kiss you in the next five minutes, I may go stark raving mad. How am I doing?" He'd taken her by the shoulders and was searching her eyes for an answer.

"You're changing the rules again," she warned.

"To hell with the rules. This isn't some game. It's life, and I'm tired of making do with fantasies. Will you come in?"

"I'd like that very much," she murmured, and stroked his jaw with her thumb.

They entered the house through the back and came into the large old-fashioned kitchen. The housekeeper had left a light burning over the sink, and it lit their way down the pantry hallway, which led into the formal dining room. In the ornately paneled foyer, where a low-watt Tiffany lamp provided the only illumination, Josh flicked a wall switch and the huge chandelier sprang to light. "I want to see you when I kiss you," he whispered as he pulled her hard against his chest and captured her face in his hands.

Marlo realized she'd been holding her breath, and she let it out in a soft breeze that fanned his face and made his eyes focus on her pursed lips. Their mutual longing was so evident, so palpable, that she expected his lips to be hard and bruising when they finally covered hers. But they were tentative and soft, almost shyly seeking her permission to deepen the contact.

When she silently gave him that permission by opening her lips, he didn't wait. For the next several minutes they explored the taste of each other, allowing their fingers to memorize the outline of each other's face while their tongues danced and probed to discover secret places that might give pleasure. Neither willingly released the kiss fully, but rather each continued to blindly read the other's expression by planting soft kisses on eyelids and cheekbones and earlobes.

"Marlo," Josh finally groaned, then eased her coat down her arms and tossed it and his own coat lightly in the direction of a tapestried seventeenth-century bench. He took her hand and led her toward the library.

"Josh." She held back, willing him to stop. "Take me to your rooms." The library was obviously the domain of business and his grandfather. Even though the older man was hundreds of miles away, she wanted Josh to concentrate totally on her tonight with no doubts.

He looked into the dark room and seemed to understand her unspoken reservations. He closed the heavy oak doors in a gesture symbolic of his silent pledge that for tonight there would be no intrusion of business or family. He lifted her in his arms and started for the wide, curving stairway. "Trust me, Marlo," he whispered. "We aren't going to do anything you aren't ready for."

She almost laughed, thinking, *Aren't ready for?* She remembered the days and weeks of working so closely with him without being able to touch him or explore the desire she felt growing each time she saw him. She tightened her grip around his neck and nestled her face in the curve of his shoulder. He quickened his step, and she could feel his heart beating against her breast.

His section of the house—the only part Sally had never shown her—was in a wing of its own. It was actually a small apartment with its own living room and small kitchen. Josh settled her on the large overstuffed couch, then bent to make a fire. He removed his vest and tie and rolled back the sleeves of his oxford shirt, revealing muscular forearms. He turned out the lights, then sat with his back to the sofa, pulling her hand over his shoulder and inviting her to massage his chest as they stared into the crackling fire.

She turned onto her side in order to fit more closely against him and to cradle his head as close as possible to her breasts.

"It's been a rough week," he said, lifting her hand to nibble her fingers and kiss her palm.

No business, she pleaded silently.

He continued when she didn't say anything. "Mostly because of being with you without being able to *really* be with you."

He waited again for her answer, and when none came, he half turned to look at her. "I've been a damned idiot, Marlo. I've wanted to be with you like this every night after work. I've even wanted to be with you like this *at* the store." He chuckled softly. "There've been so many times in the weeks since you've come into my life that I've found myself turning to you, seeking your smile, depending on your encouragement. You make me feel as if anything is possible—even that I can actually make Carrington's the business it once was.''

"It can be," she said with conviction. "It will be. And it's because of what you'd done long before I ever came on the scene. After all, the only thing I'm providing is 'window dressing.''"

He groaned at her pun, and she felt him relax even more. She felt the bonds of their friendship more certainly than ever before, and it occurred to her that this was a friendship they'd forged almost in spite of themselves. She'd certainly had no intentions of becoming involved with someone in Milwaukee. After all, she'd be going back to New York and her career. And Josh had held himself apart from any real involvement for so long that it was a miracle he could accept any level of a relationship that went beyond the bounds of a casual acquaintance of his own self-imposed limits.

"One thing I've thought about a lot since you came is how much of a loner I've always been," he said as if he could read her thoughts. "When I was a boy, my parents always seemed to be off to Europe or somewhere, racing cars or appearing on stage. J.P. and I spent a lot of time together, and I think we both recognized that we were cut from the same cloth—stubborn, self-reliant, too easily hurt and too proud to admit it. I spent so much time with him that I think subconsciously I became him. In a way he's had a pretty hard life."

"How so?" Marlo sat up to knead the tense muscles that bunched at the back of his neck.

"My father was his second child. There was another son—Alexander—who was the true heir apparent. The family structure was like that of old European days—the firstborn took care of the family business and the second child was indulged. Alex started in the stockroom of Carrington's as a boy and had worked his way through every department by the time he was twenty. At thirty he was working side by side with J.P.—equal partners. It was both their dreams come true. Alex loved the business as much as the old man did, and the two of them barely even noticed the direction my father's life took."

"And then?"

"There was an accident. Alex and my grandmother were returning from a buying trip in New York. It was winter, and there was a storm. They were flying in a private plane they'd rented in order to be home for Christmas. There were no survivors."

"Oh, Joshua, how awful for him, losing them both like that!" Marlo's heart nearly broke as she thought of the older man and his enormous loss.

Joshua nodded. "Awful for him. Awful for my father. Awful..." He let it drop.

"For you?" Marlo ventured.

"It comes off like 'poor little rich kid,' and I don't want to give you the wrong idea. I had a wonderful childhood, Marlo. I was lucky enough to live in a three-generation household. These rooms belonged to my Uncle Alex. You've seen our family wing, and my grandparents had the part in the center that overlooks my grandmother's garden."

"It almost sounds as if you had three sets of parents," Marlo said. "At least three fathers."

"In some ways I did, and each of them contributed something unique."

"What did your father contribute?"

"My father was absolutely devoted to pleasure before business." He smiled.

"Somehow that part of you seems to have gotten lost," Marlo commented, though she knew she was pressing.

"Perhaps it wasn't as indelibly stamped as the traits of duty and loyalty were," he mused. "My most vivid memories of my father are from those years after Alex died. My father was tied here to this house and the business. J.P.'s stroke practically guaranteed that. He'd always been so free to do as he pleased. It must have seemed like a prison to him. I remember him from those years as grim-faced and short-tempered. He was truly happy only when he was able to escape for a few days and sail his boat or race his cars."

He was quiet for a while, lost in private memories. Marlo continued to work at the now relaxing muscles along his shoulders, neck and upper arms. "I'd better stir the fire," he said after a few minutes. It felt to Marlo as if they'd spent many evenings like this—talking and not talking, being together.

Marlo watched his features being lit by the fire as he fanned it with the bellows until the new log caught and burned in leaping flames that were reflected around the high walls of the room. Since they'd entered his private domain her feelings for him had changed—going from raging desire to an almost fierce need to simply be with him, in bed and out. When he turned from ministering to the fire, she held out her arms and he came into them willingly, settling himself next to her on the sofa and pulling her into an embrace that spoke of his own longings.

Their kisses ran the gamut from ones that were slow and tender to those that threatened to devour their very souls. At some point Marlo released the buttons on his shirt and pulled it free of his waistband. He got out of it and returned to her arms, inviting her to explore his chest and shoulders and back. For a moment his hands were still as he savored the feeling of her touching him, his eyes closed as if trying to memorize that touch.

When she gently kissed him again on his full lips, he drew her under him and the evidence of his desire pressed against her thigh. His kiss demanded total capitulation as he probed his tongue deeper into her. Marlo could no longer distinguish between her own ragged breaths and his.

"Come here," he whispered, pulling her to a standing position. She faced him, roaming her hands over his bare chest while he opened the zipper of her jump suit as if he were untying the ribbons of a precious gift. He pushed the fabric away to reveal first her white shoulders and then her full breasts, which a moment before had strained against the confines of the garment. When the suit was past her arms, Josh let it fall in a puddle around her feet and took one long, shuddering breath as he knelt to help her step out of it completely.

He lightly caressed her calves and thighs as he took an excruciatingly long time to stand up again. As he skimmed his hands lightly over her hips and stomach, she held her breath in anticipation, aching for the moment when he would hook his thumbs under the elastic of her lace panties and take them away. She was trembling with yearning for him, and balanced herself by holding on to his shoulders. But he didn't pause to remove her undergarment, and all Marlo felt was a heightened desire and surprise and disappointment.

As if reading her expression, he smiled. "We'll get there," he promised. He pulled a patchwork quilt from the back of the sofa and spread it on the floor near the fire. From his kneeling position, he took a moment to stir the fire and add a large birch log, which crackled and split its dried bark in an imitation of fireworks on the Fourth of July. Then, still kneeling, he turned to look up at her and pull her down beside him.

"Do you have any idea how exciting you are?" He continued to stroke her thigh, and bent his head to nibble a vulnerable spot he'd discovered in the crook of her neck. Instinctively she buried her hands in his hair and drew his face closer to relieve the sweet agony his kisses aroused. But she was about to discover that Joshua could find dozens of vulnerable spots to torture. He began by teasing one nipple through the fabric of her bra. When he closed his mouth over it and stroked the tip with his tongue, Marlo thought she would go insane. But he refused to be stopped until the whole cup of her bra was damp and clinging to her body, giving her little relief from her longing to tear the fabric away and beg him to take her with no barriers.

"Joshua," she pleaded, placing her hands on his hips and urging him still closer. But he resisted, turning slightly so that her hands slipped around to rediscover the evidence of his passion. She was startled and thrilled by the power she felt there, so much so that at first she withdrew.

"Touch me," he moaned, firmly placing her hand there. "I need so much to feel you touching me, Marlo." Satisfied that she would stay there, stroking and touching him through his slacks, he released the catch of her bra and pushed it away, lowering his head to give special attention to the breast he'd neglected before.

Marlo couldn't remember ever having felt such a level of excitement. His arousal fed her desire, and for the first time in her life she felt the full power of her body both to take and give pleasure. As she released the buckle of his belt, the image of dressing and undressing the mannequins in the store came to mind. Opening the button on the slacks, pulling down the zipper—she'd done this dozens of times. But Josh was no mannequin; he was flesh and passion. He lifted his hips to allow her to push away the slacks and briefs and stopped his assault on her breasts to lie back and enjoy her undressing him.

On her knees now, Marlo worked to remove the rest of his clothing. Then she straddled his thighs and used both hands to stroke the length of him. She smiled at his murmurs and moved up his body, testing her effect on his flat nipples with her thumbs. She used her tongue to give sweet punishment to the inside of one ear until she felt him weaken and found herself on her back, with him over her. He took her mouth in a kiss so filled with heat that the fire behind them became unnecessary.

"My turn," he rasped, and finished undressing her with an urgency that mirrored her own feelings. He found her moist center with his fingers and began stroking her gently. She lifted her hips to invite more intensity, but he kept his touch light. When she was certain she wouldn't be able to take another breath, he delved his fingers deeper and deeper and stroked her more forcefully.

"Josh, I want you inside me—please," she begged, and tugged at his hips, urging them down on her own.

Hardly missing a beat, he replaced his rhythmic fingers with that part of him she'd hungered for, and her breath came in a rush as she closed tightly around him and matched his powerful cadence. Their open mouths met in a kiss that imitated the pulsation their bodies had set in motion. They drew each other more securely into the dance, and Marlo lifted her hips, seeking to take him more completely inside her.

And Josh matched her need. Never had he felt such fire, and Marlo was his fuel. He watched her beneath him, wanting to experience the moment of her climax, to be a part of that explosion, which he knew would glaze her eyes and force the breath from her. He just prayed that he could hold on long enough so he wasn't lost in the sweet agony of his own release. He cried her name when he felt her shudder, and together they rose on the crest of their ecstasy.

The room was quiet except for the occasional pop of a spark from the fire. They lay languidly together, exchanging light caresses and tiny kisses and the silence of their shared experience. They drowsily murmured their praise of each other's power to give pleasure, and sometime later they slept, curled together in each other's arms, with his leg protectively over hers and her small dark head a perfect fit in the haven of his shoulder.

Marlo was the first to awaken. It was dark and cold in the room. The fire had been reduced to a few embers that flickered and glowed, a memory of the passion they'd shared. Josh was sound asleep next to her. His lips were slightly parted, and she could feel the warmth of his breath against her face. When she stirred, he made a small sound and huddled closer to her. She got up, found his shirt and wrapped herself in it, and then pulled the quilt over Josh.

She gathered her clothing and found the bathroom. She showered, reliving in detail his hands on her, the feel of his body touching hers. She had imagined for weeks what it might be like. At the oddest times she would find herself studying the curve of his smile, the texture of his hands, and had fantasized about his caresses. Now she knew, and just the memory was arousing. Their lovemaking had been the abandonment of all the practical conservatism she'd come to expect from Josh in every phase of his life. She'd imagined that love with him would be tentative and cautious. But his uninhibited passion had stunned and delighted her. She'd never felt more totally a woman than while she was in his arms.

Something else pleased her as well. The fact that Josh had opened a part of himself and his past to her demonstrated that she was becoming more to him than just someone to have a casual affair with. Not that Josh seemed the type to simply meet physical needs. But she might have had her doubts about what he thought of her if he'd simply carried her to his rooms and ravaged her without a word. The fact that he'd wanted to tell her about himself said a great deal about what she'd come to mean to him. In these past weeks of working closely together over such long hours, she'd seen him begin to relax around her. She'd watched his trust and admiration for her instincts grow in spite of the sexual tension that charged the room whenever they were together. She'd noticed two things: his need to keep a mask on his feelings for her during business hours had lessened, and his allowing the mask to slip with her had affected his relationships with other employees.

Though he'd always been at ease with Patrick, he now moved perfectly at ease through the store as well, as he visited with members of what was rapidly becoming his second family. Joshua was finally beginning to accept the fact that the people who worked for him admired and respected him. One of the attractions Marlo had felt for him from the beginning had been his obvious concern for his employees. But there had always been that aura of restraint, that subtle separation of himself as the employer. Now he seemed able not only to listen to their problems but to share in their humor as well. Over the past busy days, she'd frequently noticed him laughing at something a clerk or buyer had related to him.

Marlo gasped at the draft of cold air that accompanied Josh's opening the shower door. But she gasped for a different reason when she felt his fully aroused body pressing against hers. "You left me," he murmured sleepily, and pulled her firmly against him under the warmth of the spray.

"It's almost dawn," she said in a husky voice. "Some of us have to go to work."

"I'm beginning to hate that guy you work for, lady."

She laughed and saw that he was only feigning sleepiness. He was wide-awake, and he wanted her again. And she knew that Joshua Carrington III usually got what he wanted.

Hours later she awoke to find herself wrapped in a down comforter in the middle of his huge bed. She remembered that he had left her with orders that she was to take the morning off, while he went in to the store, and then meet him for lunch at The Coffee Trader.

"After that," he'd whispered, "we're both going to take the afternoon off and spend it right here."

Marlo couldn't stop smiling as she hastily dressed and returned to her own apartment to change for lunch. The place seemed cold and lonely, reminding her of the way she sometimes felt when she came home to her place in New York. How many times she'd wished that she could come home to someone. Though she had dozens of friends, not to mention her family, she still vividly recalled how lonely it could be. She realized now that possibly one of the reasons she buried herself in work was that she was trying to compensate for other voids in her life. It wasn't that she was unhappy in New York—she'd never lived anywhere else until now. Certainly for all its problems there was no more exciting city on earth. And yet . . .

Face it, Fletcher, she thought. You're becoming attached to this place and, more to the point, to someone in this place.

Marlo had never really been in love before. She wasn't exactly without a history of romantic attachments, of course. But her feelings for Josh were different. She acknowledged that finally making love with him had in no way taken the edge off her need to be with him, to talk with him, to share her thoughts with him, to be quiet with him. She had always found being with him a pleasure. His intelligence and subtle wit continually delighted her. But after last night, she thought with a wry grin, I'm beginning to realize that Joshua Carrington can delight me in any number of ways.

# Seven

The party to celebrate J.P.'s birthday and the spring opening of Carrington's was scheduled for Thursday. To that end, the store was closed during the first part of the week as the entire staff worked to put the plan for Carrington's new look into action. It was an exciting, exhausting week during which every department of the store was turned upside down, inside out, and in some cases moved to another floor altogether. The employees were soon caught up in the spirit of the changes, and they were looking forward to the party as much as those who'd paid to attend what promised to be the social event of the season.

J.P. and Sally were due back from Florida on Wednesday, and Marlo could see Josh's anxiety grow as the day approached. His temper shortened in direct proportion to the amount of time left. During the final days, Marlo worked with him around the clock. They'd taken to spending every night in Marlo's apartment or Josh's rooms. But during the week before the opening, Josh more often than not grabbed a nap on the sofa in his office and Marlo went home at midday to catch a couple of hours' sleep before returning to the store in the late afternoon.

On the afternoon of the party Patrick arrived at noon and announced that he and the store were in as good a shape as they could be. "I have come," he said dramatically, "to take my rightful place in the limelight." Then, with a twinkle in his eye, he collected Josh and Marlo from their respective offices and brought them to the main entrance of the store, where a chilled bottle of the best imported champagne and three glasses were waiting. "We made it, troops!" he announced, opening the bottle with a flourish.

The tiny worry lines etched between Josh's eyes deepened. "We're not there yet," he said as he accepted a glass of champagne and glanced around.

"But we've made the first hurdle," Marlo said, and continued when she got no response. "Joshua, look at this place. It's fantastic—beyond anything we'd planned."

"I have to agree with you there," Josh said with a hint of a smile. He walked around the area, sipping his drink and taking in everything from the bouquets of black, silver and pink silk flowers to the art deco accents around which Marlo had created her displays. "You're right," he said finally, turning back to face the two of them with a full-grown grin. "Here's to the best merchandising team this town has ever seen."

"This town?" Patrick protested in mock offense. "What about this country, this continent, this universe?"

"I'll drink to that," Marlo said, and drained her glass.

"Easy there, lady. You have an entire evening of toasts and compliments to get through," Josh teased her.

"I'm ready," Marlo announced, holding out her glass for a refill.

When she got to her apartment to change for the party, Marlo's phone was ringing. As she fumbled with the lock on the heavy oak door, Marlo was reminded of another ringing phone and another day months before, in New York. Back then she couldn't have imagined anything she wanted more than to design a show for some punk producer. Her coming to Milwaukee had proved she could be happy in other places, doing other things.

She picked up the receiver on the third ring. "Marlo Fletcher."

"Marlo. Where the hell have you been for the last three days? I've been calling nonstop." The voice of her friend Manny barked over the line from New York.

"I've been working," Marlo replied. "How are you, Manny?"

"Around the clock? I've heard of the Midwestern work ethic, but that's a bit excessive, don't you think?"

"It's an opening, Manny. You know how those go."

"Theater? You're doing a show? Why didn't you let me know? I wouldn't have lined up Central Park for you."

"It's not a play, Manny. It's the opening— What did you say about Central Park?" Suddenly Marlo was on full alert.

"Central Park Summer Season. Aren't you keeping up with the trades? Gordon Madison is producing a summer season— in Central Park."

"Gordon Madison?" It was one of the biggest names in New York and London theater circles.

"That's it. And if you get your buns back here in the next three days with a decent portfolio, you can probably capture the designer spot for the season."

"Manny..." She almost whispered his name as she tried to digest what he was saying. Merely scrubbing floors for Gordon Madison was the break every theater hopeful waited for, but designing three shows for him...? "How did you do this?"

Her friend chuckled, knowing that now he had her undivided attention. "I'm in the company," he said, "and I heard them talking about the fact that the young guy they wanted had left on the red-eye for Hollywood, so I mentioned that I might know someone—"

"Manny..." she said warningly, knowing her friend had a habit of exaggerating.

"Okay. But I did mention your name to the stage manager, and the guy remembered your work on that bomb in the Village a couple of years ago. Also, Madison wants all fresh names for his park season. He's into making discoveries."

"Am I to be his latest discovery?"

"Among others. He's building the season around unknowns with talent, then he'll take the credit for making them the fresh young faces of the business. Everybody has their ego trip—this is his."

"What's the deal?" Marlo asked, noticing that time was flying and she still needed to bathe and dress for the evening. Still, this was the phone call of a lifetime where her career was concerned. The thrill of hearing her name and Gordon Madison's mentioned in the same breath was heady stuff.

"The season will be three plays in repertory—all classics. He's going to set the schedule Monday. Opening night is set for the middle of june, with the usual hoopla and dignitaries. He needs finished design sketches in three weeks. If you come Monday with portfolio and some roughs, I can set a meeting with the stage manager and Madison for that afternoon."

"I can't do this on such short notice, Manny," she wailed, thinking of the hours of sleep she'd already missed, of the hours she and Josh had looked forward to spending with each other once the opening was history. "Can't you stall things a couple of days?"

"Then you'll do it?" Manny ignored her plea.

"Well, of course I want to do it, Manny, but Monday. . ."

"Make it Wednesday, then," he offered magnanimously.

"Manny, you never had a meeting for Monday at all."

"Nope. But I had to make sure you hadn't gone all soft and decided to take up farming or churning butter or whatever they do for a living out there."

"It's not another planet, you know. Milwaukee happens to be a very cosmopolitan city." Marlo surprised not only Manny but herself as she fiercely defended the Midwest. "It has its attractions, believe me."

"What's his name? Come on, Marlo. Tell me you're not going to chuck your chance at the big time for some farmer," Manny complained.

"He's not a farmer," Marlo bit out the words before she had a chance to think. "Never mind that," she went on, exasperation clear in every syllable. "I'll be there Wednesday at four, all right?"

"Call me the minute you land. And Marlo? Bring the A stuff." He hung up.

Marlo replaced the receiver slowly. She didn't have the time to fully savor what the call might mean for her future. Josh would be coming by for her in less than an hour, and she was a mess. Still, when she studied her reflection in the bathroom mirror, she had to admit that there was a new energy behind her tired dark eyes. The circles, which had grown deeper by the day, seemed faint now, and her mind whirled with ideas for sets for the plays Manny had mentioned.

By the time she'd done her makeup and hair, Marlo had made a dozen mental sketches of set designs. Now, if she could just find the time to get them on paper, she thought. She turned to the closet for her dress of the evening. A black ankle-length jersey was all she'd brought with her that was appropriate, and she hadn't had time for shopping during the hectic weeks since they'd decided to throw this little shindig for the city's elite. She hoped it would be all right and that Josh would be pleased.

A soft rap at the door stopped her in midmotion. Wrapping her terry robe tightly around her, she answered, to find Sally standing on her doorstep swathed in fur and carrying an expensive-looking dress box.

"Sally." Marlo hugged the other woman after relieving her of the box. "Welcome home."

"Thanks, darling. It's nice to be back, although I must say we really need to do something about these endless winters here." She brushed snowflakes from her coat as she shrugged out of it.

"It hasn't been so bad," Marlo said, and immediately felt the scrutiny of Josh's mother.

"If you mean that," Sally said with a delighted grin, "then my plan has worked and that son of mine has had the good sense to see that you were kept so busy you didn't have time to notice the weather."

"Well, we have been working at the store day and night."

"I'm not talking about the store and you know it, Marlo Fletcher. I've seen my son, and there's something definitely different about that man, a new...vitality, shall we say? And you, my dear, are practically glowing. Make an incurable romantic happy and tell me it's love."

Marlo fingered the box to cover her sudden embarrassment. She had been reluctant to put a label on what she and Josh had shared. Lovemaking was one thing; love was something else again. Love implied a great deal more—commitment, for one thing. Her eyes clouded as she tried to sort out the multiple feelings raging through her mind. Feelings for Josh. Feelings about Manny's call. Feelings about leaving Milwaukee and Josh to return to New York and her career.

"Uh-oh," Sally said, misreading Marlo's unhappy expression. "I've put my foot in it, haven't I? Are you two quarreling?"

"Oh, no," Marlo hastened to reassure her. "We... we've... it's been wonderful."

"Been? Past tense?" Now Sally was frowning.

"I've just had the most wonderful offer to do a summer season in Central Park for Gordon Madison," Marlo blurted out before thinking.

"I see," Sally said, and took a minute to study Marlo. "I've brought you something for tonight." She indicated the box. "I do hope it fits. It belonged to Josh's grandmother, and as I recall she was very nearly your size."

Marlo lifted the lid and pushed aside the layers of tissue paper to discover the most gorgeous beaded gown she'd ever seen. "Oh, my!" she whispered as she lifted the dress reverently from the box.

"It weighs a ton, of course, but it's the real thing, and I believe it fits tonight's theme and color scheme perfectly." Sally was certainly right about that. Most of the gown was covered in black and silver bugle beads, with bands of pink sequins to accent the neckline and hips.

"It's fabulous," Marlo breathed as she hurried to try it on. The bodice clung to her breasts, and the dress skimmed her waist and hips and ended in a handkerchief hemline somewhere around the middle of her calves.

"Black hose and strapped pumps should finish it off quite nicely, don't you think?" Sally was walking around her, taking in the fit of the gown with a critic's eye. "Yes, I think you'll be quite smashing, and—'' her flashing eyes, so like those of her son, met Marlo's ''—whatever has brought a frown to your face needs to disappear.''

''I told you,'' Marlo said, looking for her stockings and shoes. ''I've had an offer from New York.''

Sally smiled. ''My goodness, it seems like just yesterday I came over to meet my new tenant, only to discover that she thought Milwaukee was quite possibly at the end of the earth. Could it be that the glamorous and overrated New York City now seems equally far away?'' she said in a teasing voice.

''But . . .'' Marlo caught herself in midsentence. She'd been about to say, *But I don't want to leave Josh.* The revelation was clear. Her mixed emotions were explained in that one thought.

''Marlo,'' Sally said seriously as she put on her coat and headed for the door, ''if you love Joshua, love him enough to be yourself. This offer is important to you. You're acting as if you must choose between the two, and I'm here to tell you that it's quite possible for you to have your own career and ambitions and also love my son. I know. His father and I spent time apart as we pursued our respective careers, and we were very happy for many years. Now, finish dressing. Josh is nothing if not punctual. I'll see you in the library for cocktails before we go.''

What Sally said made sense, didn't it? In the modern world it should be possible to have it all. It should be possible for her and Josh to maintain a relationship regardless of where their respective careers took them. People did it all the time. It was more difficult certainly, but it could work if both parties were willing to make it work. Feeling her old self-confidence return, Marlo finished dressing.

Now all she had to do was choose the right time to talk about her New York opportunity with Josh. She couldn't understand why she was planning the moment with such caution. It wasn't as if Josh didn't expect her to go back. After all, he'd mentioned it himself that day in his office when he'd cautioned Patrick against depending on her too much to carry through on the plans she'd developed. He'd reminded Patrick that Marlo's stay was only temporary. Maybe she'd read too much into their relationship. Maybe for Josh it'd been no more than a simple romance.

"And what does that mean, Fletcher?" she said aloud to her reflection in the full-length mirror. "Does that mean for you it's been more than a simple romance?" It certainly felt like more than that.

"Marlo? Are you ready? Open the door. It's freezing out here." Josh's voice and pounding broke her stream of thought. She hadn't even heard him knock.

"Coming," she called, and after a final check in the mirror ran to open the door for him.

He stood stunned the moment he saw her and seemed frozen to the doorstep, a posture that had nothing to do with the weather. She waited as he completed a head-to-toe appraisal of her.

"Are you coming in? I thought you were freezing," she said quietly, self-conscious under his scrutiny.

"I'm coming in. The question is whether you'll ever get me to leave again." He leaned down and kissed her softly. "That dress is incredible, lady."

"It was your grandmother's," she whispered as she trailed light kisses down the curve of his jaw.

"Stop that," he warned, "or I promise we'll stay right here until I've rediscovered every inch of that luscious body that's filling out that dress so spectacularly."

"You already know every inch of that body," she teased him, and blew into his ear.

"That's it. You're in real trouble now." He scooped her up into his arms and headed for the bedroom.

"Josh, no." She laughed, knowing he wouldn't miss the opening even for the pleasure of being in bed with her. "Come on, put me down before you mess us both up." She'd noticed how handsomely he wore his tuxedo, and now she pressed her hands against the front of his pleated white shirt.

"The only reason I'm letting you go for the moment is that we're about to spend the most fabulous evening together. The gala, the compliments, the celebration, and then..."

"Then?" Marlo smiled up at him, still holding on to his shoulders.

"I'll give you one clue," he whispered, and gathered her forcefully into his arms as he lowered his head to kiss her. It was a kiss of promise—the promise of his hunger and knowledge and something more.

"Josh? They're waiting for us in the library." Marlo tilted her head to allow him access to her neck.

"I know." He sighed heavily. "But we'll get back to this."

"Promise?"

"You can carve it in stone, beautiful lady. Now, fix your face and let's go."

They joined Patrick and other managerial staff from the store for cocktails. The buyers were all buzzing about the opening and about the merchandise they were about to unveil in the evening's fashion show. Everyone exclaimed over Marlo's gown, and throughout the hour she noticed J.P. watching her.

The staff left early in order to be in place when the guest of honor arrived. A limousine would be at the house at seven to take J.P. and Sally to the store. With all the guests and staff assembled, Josh stood at the main entrance and opened the door for J.P. "Grandfather," he said after everyone had sung "Happy Birthday" and showered the older man with streamers and confetti, "welcome back to Carrington's." There was pride and emotion in his voice as he shook his mentor's hand. His handshake was that of a man who knew he'd succeeded, and in his grandfather's eyes he saw that indeed he had.

The evening was an unqualified success. Every item in the fashion show was sold, and patrons continued to place orders as the staff circulated throughout the store. One customer ordered an entire outfit as displayed on one of Marlo's mannequins.

"Easiest sale I ever made," the buyer for the designer shop confided delightedly to Marlo, squeezing her hand.

"Excuse me. I see George Garber has arrived, and I really need to speak with him about something." Marlo headed for the man whom she'd temporarily replaced. She noted with satisfaction that he looked fit and healthy. It would be easier to take off for New York on such short notice now that she could see she wouldn't be leaving Patrick and Josh in the lurch.

"Marlo, you've done wonders with this old barn. I'm jealous," George teased her with a smile.

"You're a great teacher, even from a hospital bed. George, you're looking fabulous. I hope this means you're ready to take up the reins again, because I really—"

"George, you look fantastic." Patrick joined the two of them and clapped George firmly on the back. "How do you feel?"

"I feel fine, and if I'm looking great, it's because my doctors tell me I've been able to reduce the stress quotient of my life dramatically. I'm painting again—watercolors. There're even a couple of shows that have roped me in for the summer."

"But George," Marlo interrupted him with puzzlement in every word, "I don't understand. If you're to avoid excess stress, why take on the demands of art fairs in addition to all that has to be done here?"

Now it was George's turn to look confused. He stared at her and then looked at Patrick. "Apparently you haven't discussed my retirement with Marlo. You did tell Josh, Patrick?"

"Retirement?" Marlo was stunned. Patrick had the good grace to look sheepish and he assured George that Josh was well aware of his plans to retire early.

"Would you excuse us, George? I think I should talk with Marlo privately." He took her elbow and steered her firmly toward a quiet spot near the escalators.

"Patrick Dean, what's going on here? You said temporary—a few months tops. Now I have an offer to work with Gordon Madison and you're about to tell me that you have no one to take my place?"

"I was positive that by now you'd have planned on staying," Patrick said with his charming grin. The man was maddeningly sure of himself. "I figured that you'd be so captured by the work, not to mention what's happened in your personal life—"

"Patrick, you can't go around arranging people's lives on some personal whim. I have a chance to work with the biggest producer on Broadway and you expect me to turn my back on it?"

"What about your work here?" His smile had faded, and she saw that it was beginning to sink in that she was truly furious with him.

"This," she said with a flourish of her arm, "is what I was hired to do. It's complete, and from what I've been hearing tonight, it's an unqualified smash. You hired me to get Carrington's through this opening. Well, we've done it."

"And what about Joshua?" Patrick asked quietly.

A familiar voice startled both of them. "Joshua can take care of himself." And Josh was there next to her, refusing to make eye contact, focusing all his attention on Patrick. "Excuse me for interrupting, Patrick, but our arrangement with Marlo was that the assignment would be temporary. She's certainly served us well, beyond anything we had a right to expect or even hope for. I think we've gotten so used to having her here that we forgot she really is only a visitor. She does have another life, which needs her attention. Talk to George again, Patrick. Perhaps we can work something out along the lines of a consultant or part-timer until we have a chance to interview for a replacement." He still hadn't looked directly at her, and he was refusing to receive the frantic messages she was trying to send with her eyes. "Excuse me, will you both? I see some other guests are arriving." And he was gone, moving swiftly across the store to greet Clare and her father.

Patrick looked at her with surprise. "You hadn't mentioned anything about New York to him, had you?" he asked, incredulous.

"No. The call just came an hour before he came to pick me up, and I had no chance. I was going to talk to him about it tonight when we...after we..." She allowed the sentence to hang in the air as she studied Joshua from across the room. She noticed that he had reverted to the politely attentive but closed and aloof man he was when they'd first met. She knew then that in these past few minutes any ground she'd gained in having him live spontaneously had been lost. She had to talk to him and make him understand, and without another word to Patrick she started determinedly across the room.

But when she reached his side, he drew her into the circle of conversation. He introduced her as a respected design consult-

ant who was enormously responsible for the success of the
evening and who was now about to take her talents back to
Broadway, where she'd have the audience she deserved. There
was no warmth or intimacy in the smile he gave her. There was
only professional courtesy and hurt.

"Marlo, could I ask a favor? Please, check with the caterer
and ask him to replenish the champagne. We seem to be running low." Without waiting for Marlo's answer, he escorted
Clare onto the dance floor.

# Eight

———

When Josh refused to talk to her privately during or after the party, she tried to see him in his office on Friday. But there he armed himself with the presence of Patrick. Patrick at least had the good grace to look uncomfortable. As if Josh feared that Patrick might not be enough, he'd asked some of the senior staff to join the meeting.

"Marlo will be leaving us shortly to return to New York and her own career of stage design. I knew that each of you, as members of the senior staff, would want to join Patrick and me in expressing our appreciation for the way Marlo has played a key role in the revitalization of Carrington's. Certainly none of us could have done this alone, but Ms. Fletcher's contributions were truly extraordinary. Thank you, Marlo, on behalf of all of us." And then, to her consternation, he gave her a firm handshake and presented her with a small gift-wrapped box while the rest of the staff applauded.

Afterward there was coffee and cake, and each staff member wanted to speak with her personally. She saw Josh say something to Patrick and then gather his papers and briefcase and stride toward her. "Marlo. The very best to you. You have a great deal of talent and the personality to see that talent through to success. Thank you again for . . ." Here, at least, he faltered. "For everything." And then he was gone.

It was nearly an hour and a half later by the time Marlo could gracefully make her own exit. She wanted to talk with Josh in private. When Marlo reached the house that afternoon, she was seething. Certainly he couldn't run away from her when they lived in the same house. She rang the bell at the mansion's front entrance. After Sally had opened the door to her, she strode to the center of the foyer and announced that she had come to speak with Josh. She hoped her voice would carry up the staircase to his rooms.

"I'm afraid you'll have rather a long wait, Marlo dear," Sally said quietly, her expression alternating between amusement and concern. "Josh just left for the weekend, to stay at our cottage up near the Canadian border. You just missed him."

"Alone?" It was the first question that popped into her head. She had a sudden vision of a fair-haired country club beauty snuggled cozily next to him in some rustic cabin.

Amusement won out, and Sally smiled openly. "Yes, dear, he's quite alone, and I would say quite lonely as well. Why don't you come into the library for some sherry, and let's talk about your next move. J.P. and I can't for the life of us figure out what has happened, and we haven't been able to get a clue from Joshua."

As they turned, Marlo nearly collided with Josh as he came striding through the house from the kitchen. "I left my brief-case," he muttered, and headed for the stairs.

Marlo was no more than a step behind him. "Just a minute, Joshua Carrington. We have some talking to do." She took the stairs two at a time in order to keep up with him. By the time she reached the top, she was slightly breathless from the exertion and her own anger.

His silence was her only answer. She continued to follow him into the bedroom, where his bulging briefcase lay on the bed they had shared for those wonderful weeks, which now seemed part of another lifetime. "Will you please stand still and talk to me!" she shouted.

He paused but didn't look at her. "I don't think we have anything to talk about," he said, and waited.

"Well, I do. I'm sorry I didn't talk to you first. I fully intended to tell you, but George and Patrick sprang their little surprise on me—which, by the way, I assume you also knew about and failed to mention." She took a deep breath after her tirade.

"If you're referring to George's early retirement, I was certainly aware of that, yes."

"And you didn't find time to mention that to me?"

"That was Patrick's job. I knew he would take care of it. Neither of us felt there was any urgency. After all, it's my understanding that Patrick had hired you for six months—it's hardly been six months." It was the first sign of any emotion on his part, and at this point she'd grab at any sarcasm or bitterness that might keep him talking.

"Patrick hired me for six months or until George was well—whichever came first. George looked fine last night. I assumed—"

"But you had already decided to accept the show before you saw George last night, so his health is really beside the point, isn't it?" Despite Josh's casual attire and the inappropriate surroundings, he was the president of a successful business. Clearly she was the errant employee who was causing him problems and taking his time.

"That's true," she admitted grudgingly, "but I certainly had no intention of leaving the store high and dry. I was so happy to see George looking so well. It seemed—"

"Like an answer to your dilemma, I'm sure," Josh finished for her, and picked up his briefcase. "It's understandable that you'd want to return to New York and your life there, Marlo. I mean that. I don't want to fight with you about it. I'd like us to part amicably and get on with our lives. Now, please excuse me. I have a long drive ahead of me."

"You're unbelievable," she whispered at his retreating back. The change in her tone stopped him. "I mean, you're talking as if the only problem here is a business misunderstanding. What about us? What about what we have—or is that *had*?

Doesn't that deserve a little more than 'thank you very much for all your time and effort'?''

She saw his shoulders slump slightly, and he turned back to her—but kept his position of leave-taking. "And what's the point, Marlo? Will you stay? Will you forget about New York and the show and stay here and continue our life and our work here?"

"*Our* work! Josh, the store isn't *my* work. I'm a theatrical designer. Should I ask you to come to New York, give up the store and become a stagehand for one of my productions?"

He swept the air impatiently with his hand. "It's hardly the same thing."

"It's exactly the same thing!" She was back to shouting.

There was silence in the room for a moment.

"Marlo, I know you don't believe this right at the moment, but I'm really trying to handle this in the best way possible for both of us. Please don't make it more difficult than it already is."

"By running away from me and our problems? That's the way you're going to handle it. Well, of course, that's the way you always handle emotions, isn't it? Shut down. Put the mask in place and go stoically on. Well, let me tell you something, Joshua Carrington. I love you, and that means I'm ready to fight for what we've built. But it takes two." At her declaration, she was rewarded by a look of surprise in his eyes.

"If you love me, then stay here and be with me," he said quietly.

"I can't do that. Life and relationships carry no guarantees. My love for you has nothing to do with my wanting to go to New York and do these designs. That trip is *not* going to change in any way what I feel for you. It *is* going to change what can happen in my career in the future."

"Right," he growled, "it'll mean more shows in more cities and more time away."

"That doesn't mean I'm leaving you," she wailed.

"It's a pretty damned good imitation, then," he roared back. It was the first sign of real anger and emotion he'd shown, but within seconds he was back in control, the mask firmly in place.

"Who's leaving first?" she challenged him, and was met with silence and his refusal to face her. "If bowing out without a fight is the only way you can handle what you think is rejection, then perhaps you're right. Perhaps what we had isn't what I thought it was—at least for you. I'm going to New York, Josh, because it's important to me. And the way I see it, that should make it important to you. Life is a business, too—a business of give and take."

She walked past him and down the staircase. Sally was hovering anxiously at the foot of the stairs. But Marlo simply nodded and let herself out the door.

Marlo's unfettered spirit was the first thing about her that Josh had fallen in love with. She wasn't one to sulk or pout when she saw something that she didn't agree with. She addressed the problem in her energetic, forthright manner, and her frankness was always backed up with that smile and charming way of lifting her shoulders to accent a point. He'd been helpless from the beginning against her particular brand of logic. During the weeks they'd spent together—in bed and out—he'd never enjoyed life so much, never felt freer, yet still in control of his own life.

When she was gone, he discovered that the loss was beyond any he'd known before. His acquired discipline had stood him in good stead when his parents had left him as a boy to be raised mostly by housekeepers and his grandparents. When his grandmother and beloved uncle had been killed in the plane crash, young Josh had done a masterful job of controlling his emotions in a manner he thought his parents and grandfather would deem mature. And Josh had remained stoic even when word had come from Europe of his father's death.

Only when he realized that his grandfather was turning to him to carry on the tradition of the store, had he flinched under the weight of responsibility. J.P. had seen his hesitation and taken it for the weakness of the father visited on the son. Bitter and disappointed, he'd withdrawn his financial and emotional support and challenged Josh to prove to him and to the world that he was indeed worthy of such a task.

At that moment Josh had felt anger. Wasn't it enough that he'd served as son in the absence of his father and uncle? That he'd been loyal to the traditions his grandfather had established? That he'd returned to Milwaukee from college to take his position in the family business? When, he'd wondered, would he earn the respect that was rightfully his? When would he be accepted for himself and not merely as an extension of the line?

That moment had come, somewhat unexpectedly, at the gala and surprise birthday party for J.P. at the store. Josh had been inordinately anxious about his grandfather's reactions to what he and Patrick and Marlo had done with the family business. After all, even though J.P. had seen the ideas on paper, it was quite another matter for him to see them in reality. Josh had spent the entire day of the party rechecking every detail, trying to see the store through the eyes of its founder—J. P. Carrington.

Josh had been far too critical of himself, for the moment the wheelchair was inside the main entrance, J.P. had seen that Josh and Patrick and Marlo had accomplished a renovation that was far beyond anything the older man had anticipated. When his grandfather had accepted his welcome, there had been a fierce pride behind the gray eyes, and the older man's firm handshake spoke volumes.

As a matter of fact, Josh had been on his way to share his triumph with Marlo when he'd overheard her revealing to Patrick her plans to return to New York. In that moment Josh had understood what coming down from a drug high might be like. He'd known all along that Marlo was under the impression her work at Carrington's was temporary, but he just hadn't thought she'd see their personal relationship in the same light.

And so he'd wished her well and arranged the farewell party in his office. To have seen her alone would have been to mastermind his own undoing, so he'd fought it.

But Marlo Fletcher was not to be so easily dealt with through discipline and solitude. Her spirit remained to torment him long after she'd flown out of his life. He'd be in the store or in his rooms when he would unexpectedly smell her perfume. And then he would realize that he was making a detour through the

Carrington Woman department. Her musk perfume was sold
in that department, its mystery enhancing the unorthodox trend
of the clothes there—the clothes so like those worn by Marlo.

Marlo had been back in New York for nearly two weeks, but
it seemed like months. She'd helped Sheila move to a place of
her own, and she'd been touched when Sheila had insisted she
keep a small portable television. "You really saved my life by
letting me sublet, Marlo. It gave me a chance to get started here.
Please keep the TV." Marlo had finally given in.

There'd been no word from Josh. She'd thought of calling
Patrick or Sally to see how he was, but she decided that doing
so would be telling Josh that she'd eventually come back to him
on his terms. Perhaps he'd decided by now to forget her and get
back with Clare.

"Back to work, Fletcher!" she chastised herself, and bent
over her drawing board. Gordon was waiting for her designs.

Gordon Madison was hardly the arrogant egotist Marlo had
expected. As a matter of fact, he was quite charming, possess-
ing dry wit that was revealed by the constant twinkle in his ha-
zel eyes. On the one hand, he was the total professional. But he
loved acting on the spur of the moment. He and Marlo shared
a couple of afternoon adventures that had ended with dinner,
once in his palatial penthouse in the Village. But he'd made no
demands, no moves, other than an occasional understanding
hug.

Between her meetings and work she'd found time to see several members of her large family on a regular basis. That made
her time off easier. One afternoon while having lunch with her
mother she'd found herself pouring out all her pent-up feelings about the loss of Josh.

"You're very much in love with this idiot, aren't you?" Lucy
Fletcher had observed between bites of fruit salad.

"It shows, huh?"

"You could say that." Her mother had grinned. "Let's see.
I'm trying to decide whether I first realized it when your eyes
started to take on that dreamy, liquid look at the mention of

him or perhaps when I noticed the way your voice breaks into that odd quirk whenever you speak his name. . . .''

"Stop it!" Marlo had laughed. "You're beginning to sound like the dialogue from a bad play."

"Seriously, Marlo, if you love him that much, why did you accept the job here?"

"Love takes two," she'd said with a shaky grin.

"You can't mean this man isn't in love with you. I said he was an idiot, but I thought it was because he'd allowed you to leave Milwaukee."

"Let's just say the subject never came up." Marlo had sighed and polished off her sandwich. "Don't think the worst, Mom. Joshua is a fabulous man who just happens to have lived a very different life from mine. It's the old story of two different worlds." She shrugged.

"And what is it that you love so much about him, Marlo?"

"Lots of things. He has this streak of inventiveness and spontaneity just waiting to be tapped."

"Beware of relationships that are based on one person wanting to change another, Marlo," her mother had warned her.

"I don't think I'm trying to change him—changing him would mean I was trying to create something that wasn't there. His sense of fun and creativity are there—buried, perhaps—but definitely there." At the older woman's skeptical look, Marlo had hastened to continue. "As a matter of fact, I think the way Josh lives his life now is in many ways a lie. He lives his life for other people. . . to make up for the deaths of his uncle and father, to please his grandfather, to prove something to himself and all of them. You can practically see the control he struggles to maintain."

"And what are you going to do about it?"

"I'm going to wait and hope that he realizes that what we have goes beyond simple fun and games. In the meantime, I'm going to design three sets for New York's best producer."

Marlo smiled as she remembered the conversation now. She and her mother had always been good friends, and it had been some time since she'd had the opportunity to pour out her heart to her.

She made a couple of changes in a sketch and then sat back to give it one final, critical look. The doorbell startled her.

"Coming," she called, and stood on tiptoe to peer through the peephole. "Who's there?" she asked the uniformed youth who stood waiting patiently. She recognized the garb of a national parcel delivery service and opened the locks down to the chain which she kept in place. "Yes?"

"I need you to sign, ma'am." He handed her the small parcel through the crack and then followed it with a clipboard and pen. It occurred to her that in Milwaukee she would have opened the door completely—she might even have recognized the deliveryman and called him by name.

"Thank you," she said, handing back his board and pen.

The package had Carrington's return address, and the box inside carried the store's distinctive gift wrap. Marlo's hands shook slightly as she unwrapped the small box. She recognized it as the farewell gift Josh had handed her in front of the others at his hastily arranged party. The box yielded a note and a velvet jewelry box. She held the jewelry case in one hand while she unfolded the note.

The stationery was heavy gray vellum, and she recognized the bold strokes of Josh's handwriting. She read through the message once quickly and then read it again, trying to gauge its tone as well as search it for any hidden messages.

Marlo—

In your excitement you seem to have left this on my desk. Since I've been at the cabin for several days, it didn't turn up until now. I'm sorry not to have gotten it to you earlier and hope you enjoy it. We're all thinking of you here at the store—your work is a constant reminder of how lucky we were to have had you with us even for such a brief time. Sally and J.P. send their best regards. We're anxious to hear about you and the plays.

Best—
Josh

No matter how many times she read it through, the note gave no clues. Josh's feelings, buried between the layers of polite professionalism, remained a mystery. Was there anger? Regret? Loneliness?

She put the note aside and opened the stiff hinged top of the velvet box. On top of whatever lay inside was a small hand-lettered note that read, " 'We' think that you're . . ." When she picked up the note she discovered a gold charm that read #1. The numeral was set with three small diamonds. She glanced back at the note and saw the quotation marks around the pronoun *we*. She started to smile and then she laughed out loud. "The royal We," she cried happily, and clutched the note, which was more precious to her at that moment than any gold.

But then she stopped. Josh had written the note before she'd left. Perhaps he'd thought she'd open the gift immediately and would stay. Now that she was actually gone, he was probably angry or disappointed—or resigned to having lost her. To Marlo, Josh Carrington was simply the most infuriating man. But, if nothing else, Marlo was very good at going to the source and finding out for herself where she stood. Josh had once noted that she was a very direct person. He was about to find out just how direct she could be.

It was just after the dinner hour in Milwaukee and a Thursday. Marlo suspected that Josh would be in his office, working late. She dialed the store. "Carrington's," a lilting voice announced across the miles.

"Mr. Carrington's office, please," Marlo requested, tapping her foot impatiently.

"Did you wish to speak with Mr. Joshua Carrington or Mr. J. P. Carrington?"

So J.P. was spending some time back at the store, enough time to have commandeered an office. Marlo grinned with pleasure. "Mr. Joshua Carrington, please."

"Mr. Carrington's office," answered a cool, efficient voice that sounded nothing like that of Josh's secretary. "Hello?"

"Wilma?"

"Miss Perkins has left for the day. Did you wish to speak with Mr. Carrington, and if so, who's calling, please?"

"This is Marlo Fletcher, calling from New York. Is Mr. Carrington there?" And who's *this*? Marlo added silently.

"Mr. Carrington has stepped away from his desk for a time. Could I take a message?"

"Excuse me, but who is this?" The no-nonsense tones coming across the wire were a bit unnerving.

"This is Clare Thompson. I believe we met at the opening last month. May I take a message?"

Clare. Of course—it was Thursday. They were probably going for a late dinner after Josh finished his work. Suddenly Marlo's interpretation of the message in the gift note seemed way off base. Clare had been a part of Josh's life for a long time. Even while she and Josh were…together, Clare had been waiting.

She waited now. "Ms. Fletcher?"

"I'm sorry. No. There's no message. I just wanted him to know that the package he sent arrived safely today. Please give everyone my best regards, Clare." She said goodbye and hung up. Her hand was cramped from the iron grip with which she'd held the receiver when she'd heard Clare identify herself.

She went back to her drawing board and tried to work. She had, after all, chosen work, chosen to further her career. She'd expected that Josh would understand, even encourage her, but she'd been projecting that Josh would react as she would have for him, not within the confines of his own character. Perhaps her mother was right. Perhaps she *had* been trying to change him, fantasizing the way she wanted him to be instead of the way he was.

She worked until midnight without accomplishing much and then wearily undressed and went to bed. She lay awake, listening to the sounds of the city. Ordinarily the exercise was soothing and worked as a lullaby on her tensions. But not tonight. This night she didn't feel soothed. She only felt lonely. She kept remembering the bed at the Carrington house—her own and Josh's—and the sounds that accompanied falling asleep there. The phone jangled in harmony with her nerves.

"Hello," she answered with no attempt at masking the depression and tiredness in her voice.

"Marlo?"

It was Josh. The feelings that swept through her at the sound of his voice were a strange mixture of relief, exhilaration, and love. "Josh," she caressed his name in a whisper.

"Marlo, you sound terrible. Are you sick? Talk to me." His concern was like another gift. There was caring in every word.

"No, I'm fine, Josh. You didn't have to call back. I told Clare—"

"I know. I got the message. I'm just sorry it took me so long to get back to you. There was a breakdown at the store—something in the pipes—we had water all over the third floor. It was a mess. And then I hesitated because it was so late and the time difference..."

"You must be exhausted. Did you get the pipes fixed?"

"Yeah, finally...about half an hour ago."

"Clare must have been disappointed." It was out before she could stop it. It wasn't catty; it was a need to find out more about the role Clare played in his life, though Marlo knew it was uncustomarily devious of her. "Scratch that," she said. "It's a comment unworthy of response."

"Not if it displayed an edge of jealousy," he said quietly.

"How are Sally and J.P.?"

"Mom's the same—firmly in charge of both our lives. And J.P. is back at the store part-time and thriving on it. And you changed the subject."

"What was the subject?"

"Clare. Or more to the point—Clare and I. The answer is that Clare and I are just good friends. In truth, that's all we ever were."

There was a pause.

"I got the charm. Thank you." For a person who babbled on at the drop of a hat, Marlo was having an inordinately hard time trying to carry on this conversation.

"You were pretty anxious to get out of here. I figured you had just forgotten to take it along."

"It's very...special."

"Marlo. Stop being so hesitant. What's going on?"

She exhaled and let out with the breath some of the hurt and loneliness she'd kept reined in for the past two weeks. "I thought you'd be happy for me when this job came along. No one had ever hinted that the position at the store was anything other than an emergency fix to get you guys through the spring gala. And when you refused to discuss it, it was as if you were telling me there was a choice to be made. I don't think I should have to choose. There's no reason on earth why I shouldn't be able to have both my career and a relationship with you."

"You'll just have to take my word for it that from my experience such arrangements don't work very well," he answered with maddening calm.

"Well, it's been my experience, Josh Carrington, that trying to live your life on the basis of what you think other people want or on the basis of how other people have lived theirs doesn't work at all," she replied tersely.

"I don't want to fight with you long-distance," he muttered.

"Then come out here and do it in person," she challenged.

And then there was silence as each waited for the other.

"How are the rehearsals going?" he asked in a softer tone.

"Now who's changing the subject? No, forget that. Things are coming together. Gordon is fantastic to work with—a total professional who knows his business."

"Better than some of the 'boy wonders'?" Josh was teasing her now, reminding her of her tirade one evening about the sorry state of the theater and its preoccupation with youth.

"The boy wonders should be so lucky as to have the talent Gordon Madison has in his little finger. Anyway, the designs are almost set and we start construction next week. The crew is just waiting for my final go-ahead."

"When will you be finished?"

"It'll take several weeks—that's with no strikes or delays or other unforeseen catastrophes." Was he getting around to something? she wondered.

"And then what?"

"I don't know," she answered honestly. Ordinarily she would have automatically described her plans to line up the next job either in New York or as a guest designer for a repertory company somewhere else in the country. Uncertainty was the nature of her business. It was also the most wearing part.

"Have you thought of applying with the Rep here or with one of the other companies?"

"It crossed my mind." It had also crossed her mind that this conversation was beginning to move like a carefully choreographed dance. Each withheld full answers, waiting for the other to lead or follow.

"We'd like that—that is, Mom and J.P. and I would." She could hear the smile in his voice.

"What about you? Don't you have to be in New York soon to do some buying?"

He seemed to relax at her question and talked more easily, filling her in on what was happening at the store, how the plans they'd created together were beginning to fall into place. He colored every word with caution, but she could hear that in fact the business was doing very well.

After a long moment she heard him sigh before going on. "Look, I didn't call to talk about business. We're doing fine, but you know how I like to worry and agonize over every detail even in the best of times. It's good to talk to you, Marlo. I'm really happy for you—I mean that it's working out so well with Madison."

"Thank you." She didn't know what else to say. Ask me to come out there when I'm finished, she begged him silently. Ask if you can come here. Anything. Just show me that you need me for *you* and not the business.

"Well, it's late," he began.

He was going to hang up. I won't let it end in this mire of nauseating polite chitchat, she thought.

"Joshua?"

"Yes?" He was alert, eager for whatever she might say to him.

"Joshua, at the risk of making a complete fool of myself, I'm going to say something."

"I don't know," he teased her. "I've always thought it so charming, the way you beat around the bush."

"Right," she commented dryly, and continued. "What we shared in Milwaukee seems to me to have been something more than a casual affair." She gulped on the last word; It sounded slightly tawdry, and she'd never used it before in relation to herself. "At least from my point of view, there were feelings that went a lot deeper."

"How deep?" His voice was rough and husky.

"Deep," she repeated firmly. "I'm sorry for the way you found out about Madison's offer here. I had no intention for you to overhear that. I wanted to tell you later that night when we ... after we left the party."

"In bed?" he asked, but there was no challenge or accusation in his voice. Rather he seemed to savor the words.

"Yes," she whispered, suddenly overwhelmed with images of their lovemaking, especially the way Josh lost all trace of the conservative and practical Midwestern business executive when he was making love.

"I was hurt that you were telling Patrick before mentioning it to me," he admitted. "In a lot of ways I know I overreacted, but there was so little time and I needed to think it all through. You weren't allowing any time for that."

"Is that why you avoided me even to the point of arranging that ridiculous farewell party and dashing off to the north woods?"

"Listen, Marlo, I was pretty certain that if I saw you alone— whether it was in my office or the front window on Wisconsin Avenue—the only thing I was going to be able to do was pull you into my arms and make love to you until you couldn't even remember New York or Gordon Madison, much less leave me." There was a vehemence in his voice she hadn't heard there before.

"That might have been fun," she answered, letting him imagine the smile that played across her face at the fantasy of making passionate love for all Milwaukee to see in the now defunct Victorian window where they'd first met.

"So, what do you want, Josh?" Marlo asked, trying to break the silence that had traveled the wires for several moments.

"I want you back," he said huskily. "I want you to come back here and roar through my life again and upset the way I've so carefully arranged my routine. And this time I want you to stay."

"Oh, Josh, don't you understand that when I accept a design job, it doesn't mean forever? That I can be there with you and here at the same time? That we can have it all?"

"Perhaps you can, Marlo. A month in New York, then jet back here for a few weeks, and then off to L.A. or Houston or who knows where. Marlo, I need you to try to understand that for my whole life I've been surrounded by people I love who kept leaving and who sometimes didn't come back. I don't want to live that way. I don't want our children to live that way—with surrogate parents."

"*Our* children?" She was incredulous.

He brushed off the comment gruffly. "Freudian slip. You know what I mean. The point is that we're different, and I don't want to change you, but I don't think I can change for you."

"I'm not asking you to change, Josh. I'm hoping that some of the spontaneity and warmth and courage that comes with taking a risk—those qualities you show in business, those qualities we share when we make love—can be a part of the person you allow yourself to be all the time. You don't always have to hold that part in check, you know. It's okay to let go now and then—to be a free spirit. It doesn't mean you've lost control. If anything, it means you're more in control than before, because you're being yourself and not some puppet you think others expect you to be." There was a ferocity in her voice that wavered between anger and passion."

"Well?" she demanded when he remained silent.

"I have to go now. You have a big day tomorrow. It's very late, and we're both exhausted." He paused. "You have to allow me time to think, Marlo."

"Agrrrr! Stop thinking. Just feel!" she shouted. His laughter surprised her.

"Believe me, lady," he chuckled, "I'm feeling plenty. So much that I doubt one cold shower will take care of it. Break a leg tomorrow, my number-one Marlo. I'll be in touch." And he was gone.

Just like that, Marlo fumed, and mimicked his "Break a leg." Honestly, he was the most exasperating man.

# Nine

———

Josh hung up the phone and remained sitting at his desk for several minutes. His office was filled with Marlo. And when he returned to his apartment at the mansion, that was filled with Marlo as well. Just when he thought she was fading from his memory, he'd see a design she'd created or hold a meeting in which three or four people would bring up her name—"When Marlo was here, she..." or "Marlo thought..."

He'd taken to spending long hours at the store in spite of her touch everywhere, because it was preferable to returning to the house where first he had to run the gauntlet of Sally's thinly veiled probing about whether he'd been in touch with Marlo. Even J.P. had shown an inordinate interest in how Marlo was doing in New York.

When he escaped the two of them and retired to his own domain, there was little relief. The sofa, the fireplace, and especially the bed held her essence. He'd be reading the paper and suddenly find himself staring blankly at the newsprint while his mind replayed an evening when she'd decided they should try to make popcorn over the fire in the fireplace. When they'd ended up with a burnt mess, she'd been undaunted and had insisted that toasting marshmallows would be just the remedy.

He could see her sitting cross-legged before the fire, intently unbending wire coat hangers to use for sticks. She'd been dressed in a gray sweat suit that looked a hundred years old. It was paint-spattered and worn at the cuffs and collar. But it could've been an expensive ball gown for all Josh noticed. What he saw was Marlo, the tilt of her head, the sparkle in her dark eyes, the lush sweetness of her mouth.

After a few nights of memories like that, Josh had become a late-night walker along the lakefront. He slept only after he was exhausted, so in order to arrive at that state, he worked out at the gym and walked.

He also worked. In her absence he'd convinced himself that he needed to take a more active role in the actual nuts and bolts of the business. And so when the plumbing emergency had arisen on the third floor, he'd insisted on overseeing the repairs personally.

Back in his office there'd been the note from Clare: *Gave up and took myself to dinner. Marlo called to say package arrived. No other message. Josh, go find her and be happy. For once do what you want and not what everyone else wants of you—which in this case happens to be the same thing. I'll see you around. How about lunch sometime? Clare.*

They'd both known even before Marlo had arrived that their seeing each other was perhaps more of a convenience for two busy people than a basis for romance. Clare was as bright as she was beautiful. And she had too much class to continue playing second fiddle to another woman. So he'd dialed Marlo's number, which he'd committed to memory—from numerous times of picking up the phone over the past weeks and dialing right up to the last digit before hanging up.

After talking to her, he put on his coat and headed home. For once he left the bulging briefcase on his desk. Tonight he'd sleep. He let himself in the front door of the dark old house and was surprised to see a light coming from the library. It was very late and unlike either Sally or J.P. to leave a light on, once they'd retired for the night.

"Come in, Joshua," his grandfather said when Josh peered into the paneled room as he removed his overcoat. "You're later than usual tonight. You're working such long hours these days, though I wasn't aware of any situations that might require such dedication from you."

"You're right. Everything at the store is going fine—as you well know, Grandfather." Josh smiled at the older man. He decided the near disaster with the pipes could wait till morning. His delight in having J.P. back at the store even part-time was genuine. His grandfather's expertise had made the revival of the store a continuing success since he'd rejoined the staff.

J.P. sipped his brandy and motioned for Josh to take a chair close to the fire. They sat in companionable silence for a few minutes, during which J.P. said quietly, indicating the bar, "A glass of wine?" Josh shook his head, recognizing that for the first time J.P. had offered his grandson the drink of Josh's preference rather than the brandy he himself preferred.

"I would've thought we'd have heard something from Marlo by now," J.P. mused after a time. He didn't look directly at his grandson but studied the rim of his glass instead. "Just this afternoon Sally was wondering aloud how the plays were going."

"Mother wonders about Marlo every day in one way or another, and always within my hearing." Josh smiled. "Did she bribe you to stay up late tonight so I couldn't possibly make it to bed without having to discuss Marlo?"

J.P. shrugged and then added gruffly, "I'd hardly stay awake for the purpose of mentioning some girl's name in your presence, Joshua. It's just that Sally...and I...grew quite fond of the young woman. I rather enjoyed her sharp wit and direct nature."

Josh changed his mind about the wine and rose to help himself. As he sat down again he couldn't resist a small dig at his stern grandparent. "She certainly handled you once or twice."

He anticipated an impatient retort or wave of the hand and was surprised when J.P. smiled and replied, "Not nearly as effortlessly as she handled you, boy, so I wouldn't go casting laughs at others if I were you."

Josh shifted uncomfortably in his chair. J.P. continued to observe this. "I heard from her today," Josh said as he drained his glass. "She called to say she'd received the staff's farewell gift. She'd forgotten it in my office when she left and I sent it on to her...."

"You're babbling, Joshua. Get to the point. Is she coming back? How are the shows going? When are you seeing her again?"

"I don't know," Josh admitted, thinking of the tangled web they'd woven in one phone conversation about each changing for the other, about careers versus life-styles.

"Joshua," J.P. said with a great deal of exasperation, "your mother is right. We have created a robot. Do you have feelings for Marlo?"

"Well, of course..."

"Do you by some miracle recognize those feelings as the infant stages of love?"

"Yes."

"Are you planning to take any action on those feelings?"

"Of course," Josh replied brusquely, and strode back to the bar to refill his glass.

"Well, thank God for that. I'm going to bed now, so I can be awake enough in the morning to report to Sally that you're human after all and that you will indeed be taking matters into your own hands. And that Ms. Fletcher will be rejoining this household before she knows it. Good night, son."

The following morning, Patrick was not at all surprised when Josh announced his intention to spend a few days in New York, overseeing the coordination of several orders for the fall season. "Well, hallelujah," the tall blond executive said softly as he sat across from his friend. "You finally came to your senses and realized what you were about to lose. Is that it?"

"To tell you the truth, I sometimes think half the reason I'm doing this is to get you and Mother and J.P. off my back," Josh replied laughingly. There was no need to define what "doing this" meant.

"Come on, Carrington. You're in love with her, and you've been in hell since she walked through that door. Admit it, or I'll call a meeting of the senior staff and have every person who works for you tell you how this prince of a fellow who used to be their boss changed overnight into a surly, withdrawn hermit.''

Josh sank back into the high-back leather chair with a weary sigh. ''Things just haven't been the same without her, have they?''

''Are you speaking personally or in the business sense?''

''Both,'' Josh said with a smile. ''Even with all her ideas and designs in motion here, something is missing. There just isn't any... flair in anything.''

''And what isn't there for you, Josh, now that she's gone?''

''Laughter, spirit, excitement. The feeling of the wind in my face. That rush of adrenaline that comes with taking a chance on the unknown. Adventure is missing. Fun is missing. Spontaneity is missing.''

Patrick gave a low whistle and leaned across the desk to examine his friend closely. ''This is really bad. I've never seen anyone with a worse case.'' He clucked his tongue and shook his head.

''Cut it out, Pat. This isn't some frat-house romance,'' Josh said with impatience, and got up to pace his office, thrusting his hands dejectedly into the back pockets of his trousers. ''The question is how to pull this one off. How to win her back without running the risk of losing her entirely.''

''Come again? This time with a little clarity.'' Patrick was clearly confused.

Josh stopped pacing and told Patrick the gist of his phone conversation with Marlo. ''She thinks one of us will have to change for the other before we can work, and that isn't any way to start a... life together.''

''Catch-22?'' Patrick offered, and Josh nodded miserably.

''The one thing she doesn't understand is that what we have together—how we were—was real. The times I was with her and laughing and trying new things—that was being myself, dammit. It's just that I've been looked to to be strong and responsible for so long that it's become too easy to forget there's that other side of me. Hell, *I* almost forgot there *was* another side.''

"But that's only part of the problem," Patrick reminded him gently, and when Josh turned to him with raised eyebrows, he continued. "How do you feel about Marlo traveling all over the country to get work as a designer?"

Josh stopped and stared out his office window for so long that Patrick thought either he was so angry that he couldn't form an answer or that he hadn't heard the question. When the man who'd been his roommate, best friend and boss finally turned around, Patrick's heart went out to him.

"I don't know how to make her understand that for as long as I can remember, people I really cared about have been walking in and out of my life as if it were some kind of revolving door." Josh was talking quietly, almost as if he'd forgotten anyone else was in the room. "It seems that my role has always been to act as the constant for others. I'm always there, dependable, loyal . . . and waiting."

"Sounds like you might be a little angry about being taken for granted," Patrick ventured. It was the first time Josh had spoken so directly of the family life that had had such an effect on him.

"Maybe." Josh tossed the idea aside; he was too practical to be comfortable with self-psychoanalysis. "I don't know about hidden feelings and suppressed anger, Patrick. All I know is that I'm tired of going home to empty rooms and empty apartments. Why do you think I moved back to the mansion? I'm tired of living my life through this store. I'm tired of living my life through the social world that will make a difference to my business but doesn't matter a whit to me."

"Marlo might be a little tired of empty rooms herself, you know," Patrick suggested. "It's in the nature of her work that she needs to travel to the job from time to time; it's not as if that's her preference. And even if it were, just because two people are separated geographically doesn't mean they have to be apart emotionally. Don't get me wrong, Josh. I'm the last person who should be handing out advice on love, though Marlo keeps saying that one of these days some lady's going to come along and knock me off my playboy pedestal. Well, let me tell you a secret. I hope she's right, because from where I'm sitting, what you two feel right now looks pretty inviting."

"I'm miserable," Josh growled.

Patrick laughed and clapped Josh across his broad shoulders. "No, you aren't. You're in love—good, old-fashioned, head-over-heels love. The kind that screams for commitment and knot-tying and all the rest of it. Don't worry about a thing here. I'll see you when the two of you get back." He headed for the door and then turned with a devilish grin. "And Josh? It's a relief to know you're still human after all. What could be more apropos than for you, the hard-headed workaholic, to fall in love in April, when the very essence of love is in the air? Try to be original about the wedding, will you? Don't set it for June." Josh could hear his full-bellied laugh echoing down the hallway as Patrick returned to his own office.

Marlo finished her meeting with Gordon and the rest of the design staff a little past six, gathered her portfolio and started the trek home from Central Park. Spring was in the air as she strode along Fifth Avenue, observing lovers who strolled hand in hand, oblivious to the throngs of office workers and business people who jammed the streets as they rushed for the nearest subway or bus stop.

Cabbies honked furiously at other drivers as they made their way downtown, but their windows were open to capture the soft April breeze as they roared out obscenities to wayward motorists or pedestrians. Rockefeller Center was filled with potted daffodils, hyacinths and tulips, and the tables for the outdoor café were in place.

A long silver limousine passed Marlo at a crawl and then pulled to the curb half a block ahead of her. Though Marlo wasn't starstruck, she felt it was always interesting to catch a glimpse of some famous personality emerging from the luxurious extravagance of such an automobile. The silver limo pulled to a halt just as she was approaching the corner. The light was with her. She saw the chauffeur, in a dove-gray uniform, get out of the huge car and walk stiffly to the passenger side, where he opened the rear door. Marlo slowed her pace just a bit, but when she was almost abreast of the open door and no one had gotten out of the car, she hesitated, feigning interest in the contents of a shop window, until the limo's passenger had alighted.

"Ms. Fletcher?" The chauffeur tipped his hat with respect.

"Excuse me?" Marlo was certain she'd misunderstood and that the man had simply requested she move along or stop staring. Why on earth would such a person address her by name?

"Ms. Fletcher, I've been retained to see that you arrive safely home this evening and for the rest of this week. May I take your portfolio for you?" He gestured toward the worn leather pouch, which contained the final drawings for the sets.

Marlo opened her mouth, but no words emerged. She couldn't think of a thing to say except, "Who retained you?" She was so stunned at having this conversation at all that she fell into the formal tone the chauffeur had used in addressing her.

"That isn't something that I've been told, Ms. Fletcher. I assure you that my company has that information and that I've been retained to simply see that you arrive safely at..." He discreetly consulted a small white card in his pocket and then quoted her address.

"This is weird," Marlo said, eyeing him with suspicion. She wasn't about to get into a strange car—regardless of its size or appointments—with a man she'd never seen before, hired by some unknown admirer. "I prefer to walk," she said firmly, and pushed the door of the limo closed and continued on her way.

"Very well." The chauffeur accepted her decision, and with a sigh of relief she saw him get back into the limo and start the quiet, powerful motor. But she was unprepared for what followed. He paced the car to her gait. To the irritation of what seemed to be every cabbie in New York, he set the car at a speed that kept her in his view at all times. When Marlo halted and turned to glare at the driver, he pulled to the curb and once again bounded from the car to open the rear door with a flourish. People were beginning to follow her and gape.

"Let me see your credentials and the order for this...service," she demanded impatiently. "Here. Hold this," she said as she unsuccessfully tried to juggle her purse, her

portfolio and the numerous forms of identification and order
directions the driver offered. He took her portfolio without a
word and waited at attention for her to rummage through the
papers he'd offered. "Stay right there." She went to a nearby
phone, where she dialed Information and confirmed the exis-
tence and phone number of the limo company. When she called
the company and demanded to speak with the highest in command, she was transferred to a smooth-talking, ever-polite, but
entirely protective executive.

"I'm sorry, Ms. Fletcher, but a condition of the order was
that the name of the subscriber be protected. You understand,
I'm sure."

With little satisfaction other than the assurance that the
chauffeur was sincere in wanting only to follow orders and drive
her home, Marlo assessed the situation. The crowd was growing, as was their curiosity to know who she was. She'd never
liked the trappings of fame, which was one reason she'd chosen a career behind the scenes. At the moment, accepting the
ride seemed the lesser of two evils, so she climbed into the back
seat, which seemed only slightly smaller than her entire apartment, and tried not to be impressed by the smell of money and
sumptuous elegance.

"The windows stay down," she ordered, "so if you head one
block out of the direction of my apartment I can scream bloody
murder and leap out." She couldn't be certain, but it seemed as
if the driver smiled ever so slightly at her words. His eyes met
hers in the rearview mirror and he tipped his hat again.

"As you wish. Would you like to make any stops before we
arrive at your home, Ms. Fletcher? Do you need any groceri-
es, or could we pick up something for you to dine on at a restaurant along the way?"

"Just drive straight to the address on that card in your pocket
and then tell your anonymous client to call off the deal," she
said impatiently. There was another tip of the hat as he pulled
into traffic, and this time she was positive the eyes showed
laughter.

Actually the ride was a very short one. There was hardly time
for her to take in everything—the champagne on ice, the ap-

petizers tastefully arranged on a crystal platter, the color television, telephone and videotape player.

"Would you like me to carry your portfolio to your door, Ms. Fletcher?" He was standing at attention, with the door open for her exit.

"No, thank you. That will be all," she said with a tone of dismissal intended to convey that she did this sort of thing all the time. Of course, she totally spoiled the illusion with her next words. "Um, am I supposed to tip you?"

This time the driver had no success in hiding the smile that flickered across his ruddy features. "That's been taken care of, Ms. Fletcher. May I see you to your door?"

"That won't be necessary," Marlo replied, and stared at the man for several seconds, trying to make him uncomfortable. "Who hired you?"

"I'm very sorry, Ms. Fletcher, but I honestly don't know. Would you do me the kindness of allowing me to escort you to your door so that I can report to our client that his orders were followed?"

"I'll signal you from the window," Marlo said as she directed his attention to the top floor. "It's the third—" She stopped in midsentence, and she and the driver gaped at the bouquet of Mylar balloons that was dancing outside her window. "It's that one," she finished lamely as she gathered her belongings and headed for the front door of the building. The driver simply nodded. There was certainly no need for further identification.

Marlo stopped at her mailbox to retrieve the day's catch of two advertisements, a catalog from a company in Texas, and the notice for her rent.

"Fletcher," the superintendent growled at her from behind the crack he'd opened in his door. He peered distastefully at her with one bleary eye. "You'll have to clean up those balloons yourself. I don't do outside work, and that guy insisted on putting them on the outside." The door slammed before she could ask what guy, and she knew better than to seek further information.

As the ancient elevator chugged to her floor, Marlo leaned against the grilled cage and mused about the identity of her secret tormentor. Then she smiled. Of course. It had to be. *Mom*, she thought as the elevator wheezed to a stop three inches short of the top floor. Marlo climbed out and fumbled with the multiple locks until she'd gained access to her apartment. She moved to the window to alert the driver of her safe arrival and then tugged at the balloons until she was able to release them and drag them inside to float to the ceiling.

It made sense that it would be her family. Her mother and sisters had called several times a day over the past weeks, worried that she was pining away. When they'd all gotten together for Easter dinner, there'd been a lot of talk about how she wasn't eating properly and looked lousy. It was obvious where she'd come by her tendency to be direct.

"I'd love to take full credit, Marlo," her mother told her the following morning when she called. "Actually, I'm a bit jealous. The whole idea is fantastic. The driver really followed you down Fifth Avenue with a silver limo? In the middle of rush hour?" It was clear that her mother, who'd pulled more than one stunt of her own in the past, was in awe of the creator of this particular scheme.

Marlo felt a little silly, and at this moment the still unknown perpetrator was not one of her favorite subjects. She'd gleefully announced that she hadn't been fooled for a moment when the magnificent limousine had escorted her home and then been waiting politely at the curb when she'd come out of her apartment to walk to work that morning. But her mother had been strangely silent on the other end of the wire. Marlo had gone on, certain that her mother's silence was a ploy to make her doubt what she knew must be true. But finally, after describing the whole scene in detail, she'd become convinced that her mother didn't have the foggiest notion what she was talking about.

"Then who?" she wondered aloud, and frowned. Mentally she ran down the list of her friends. Some of the most likely candidates were out of town. Others were in town but hardly in a financial position to take a cab around the corner, much less hire a limo for three days. Then there was always the possibility another member of her avant-garde family...

"Well, whoever he is, the guy's got style," her sister Vicki said, when they met for a late breakfast before Vicki went to rehearsal. Vicki had been very happy to ride with Marlo in the limo, regardless of who was footing the bill.

By Friday Marlo had resigned herself to emerging from anywhere and finding the limo waiting by the curb. Each time she'd debate for just a second as she studied the driver's stoic face, and then with a sigh she'd climb into the back seat. There was no use fighting it. She had no doubt that the driver would simply follow along as he'd done before. "Do you have a name?" she asked as she flipped through one of the elegant European fashion magazines that'd been left on the back seat for her pleasure.

"James," came the reply.

Marlo almost choked on an appetizer. "Not really!" she groaned. "As in 'Home, James'?"

"Yes, ma'am."

They rode in silence, the trip taking longer in the heavy Friday traffic. Marlo was startled when the phone rang. She let it ring several times and then leaned forward. "Shouldn't you answer that, James?"

"Oh, pardon me, Ms. Fletcher. Did you want me to take your calls?"

"My calls? No one knows I'm here. It must be for you."

The phone continued to ring while James waited for instructions. "I'm quite sure the call is for you, ma'am. The agency doesn't allow personal calls for its drivers. Shall I take a message?"

"I've got it." Marlo sighed as she leaned into the plush velvet seat. "Hello?" Her tone was tentative, as if she couldn't fathom how a phone could work in a moving car.

"Hello, Marlo." It was the unexpected but all-too-familiar husky voice of Joshua Carrington.

"Carrington, how did you get this number?"

He ignored the question. "I was wondering if perhaps you would be free to join me for dinner."

The light finally dawned, and a grin broke across Marlo's wide mouth. This time she caught the driver smiling back at her, and she indicated that he should raise the partition between his front seat and her mobile phone booth.

"Actually," she said, munching loudly on a carrot stick, "I've started without you. I'm already on the first course. Care to join me?"

"That depends." She could hear the smile in his voice. "Where are you?"

Marlo peered out the window, trying to catch a street number. "Somewhere in the low Sixties or high Fifties—Fifty-ninth Street."

"Wonderful. Have the driver pick me up." He gave the name of a small elegant hotel just east of the avenue and hung up.

At Marlo's instructions, the driver swung the huge car easily through traffic to head down a side street. Within minutes he pulled to a halt in front of the hotel and jumped out to open the door for Joshua.

"Hello," said Josh. He'd meant it to come out light and charming, as if they were two characters in a drawing-room comedy. But suddenly it seemed like ages since he'd been able to feast his eyes on her, and even in the jeans and oversize yellow shirt with paint stains, she was ravishing.

"Hello? That's all you can say? Joshua Carrington, you're responsible for all of this—*plus* the balloons, *plus* my making a complete idiot of myself with practically everyone I know—aren't you?"

"If you're referring to my seeing that you go to and from work in comfort and security, I'm guilty. The balloons? Guilty. Everyone you know? I'm afraid there you've got me—I don't know what you're talking about."

They'd been staring at each other as if the moment would disappear if either broke the look while James made his way back to Fifth Avenue. Suddenly Marlo started to smile and then giggle, and then they were laughing uproariously at everything and nothing. "In my wildest dreams..." Marlo gasped.

"Oh, come on. Why wouldn't I be one to plan something like this? I'm crushed." Josh made a show of looking devastated.

"It's just—the last time I saw you—even when we spoke the other night, I thought—"

"You were wrong," he muttered, suddenly serious. "James," he said over the phone-turned-intercom, "we're expected at the North Lake Inn for dinner. But take your time getting there, please."

"Very good, sir."

"Where's the North Lake Inn? I'm not exactly dressed for anything fancy," Marlo said, trying to smooth the wrinkles from her shirt.

"It's in Connecticut, and it doesn't matter what you wear. We have a private room there." Josh was manipulating several of the dials and buttons on the console next to the telephone. "Ah, there we go." He leaned back and grinned as he watched dark tinted glass completely isolate them from James and the outside world.

"Convenient," Marlo observed wryly, trying to disguise the leap her pulse had taken the moment she realized they were to be totally alone during the time it took James to drive them to Connecticut. And since she knew James took his orders very seriously, it would probably take them at least twice the normal length of time to get there.

"Champagne?" Josh filled two glasses and handed one to her. "A toast to the success of the plays." He touched her glass with his and took a long swallow, watching her steadily over the rim.

"Thank you," she murmured, and sipped her champagne.

"Your turn," he prompted.

"Okay. A toast to the success—or should I say to the continuing success?—of Carrington's."

"Hear, hear," he said, and they drank again. "Now that we have business out of the way..." he said, taking her glass and his own and placing them in the bar at his side. He pulled her into his arms and lightly traced her features with his fingertips. "I've missed you," he said softly, kissing the outline of her ear before exploring the interior with his tongue. "You're trembling, Marlo," he whispered.

"It's just...I don't know what's coming. I don't know what you may have planned."

He pulled inches away so that he could look down at her and grinned with delight. "Well, how does it feel, Ms. Spontane-

ity, Live-for-the-Moment? What's it like to be on the receiving
end of some unpredictability for a change?''

"You're really enjoying this little game, aren't you?" She
tried to insert a note of gruffness, but failed in the presence of
his nearness, his muscular embrace, his breath on her face.

His features clouded. "I told you before, Marlo. I don't play
games. What you're seeing is just another facet of who I am."

"I see. Sort of 'what you see is what you get'?"

He smiled again and pulled her closer. "That's it."

"I like it." She nuzzled his neck and played with the buttons
on his sports shirt with her fingers. She opened the first button
and then the next until she'd cleared the way to massage the
muscles of his chest.

"And I like that," he said softly, and pulled her around until she reclined across his lap and he could kiss her thoroughly.

In that kiss was all the pain, loneliness and longing the two
of them had suppressed for weeks. Any doubt either may have
had about the seriousness of the other's feelings disappeared in
the moment of hunger and sheer passion. Neither could drink
deeply enough of the other. Neither could touch enough to
satisfy the desire that one kiss aroused.

"How I've missed you," he groaned as they parted to try to
gain some control over the pounding of their hearts and their
inability to catch a full breath. He eased his hand in a slow,
hypnotic track up her leg and around to the inside of her thigh,
coming close but never touching that place where she longed
most to be touched. Then he tenderly slid the fabric of her
oversize shirt off of her shoulder until her skin was bared for
his exploration.

Marlo groaned and strained to be closer to him, causing the
buttons on her shirt to escape their holes and the shirt to fall
away, exposing her breasts, her nipples hardened and seeking
contact with any part of him. In a moment he'd completely
undressed her from the waist up and positioned her against the
back of the wide velvet seat so he could stretch out next to her.
He cupped one breast as if it were a piece of ripe fruit that
might relieve his parched mouth. And he tasted. For long moments, Marlo lay with her eyes closed, thrilling to the variety of

sensations he awakened as he nibbled and sucked and massaged with his tongue.

She tangled her fingers in his thick hair, urging him closer and signaling her pleasure at each new stimulation. He rested his hand lightly on her stomach and then began a gentle massage that dipped lower and lower until she could feel the warm moisture building between her thighs. When she thought she'd scream if he didn't tear her jeans and his trousers away, he unsnapped and unzipped her garment and slowly pushed the tight denim down her legs as he followed its path with kisses clearly designed to stoke the fire he knew flamed within her.

When she was naked except for a pair of lace panties, she pulled away and knelt next to Josh on the carpeted floor while she undressed him with the same thrilling languor he'd used to inflame her. She smiled when she heard him moan as she opened the fly of his tailored slacks. When he was completely undressed he reached for her, but she teased him by slipping away and moving to his feet, which she massaged and kissed while he writhed and reached for her again, finally lifting her up.

Marlo balanced herself above him, allowing her breasts to tease his furry chest as she watched in fascination the way his eyes grew darker and darker, as if they were clouds of a gathering thunderstorm.

He turned her until she was trapped between him and the luxurious cushions of the huge car. She drew him to her, desiring his kiss, his touch—him. He stroked his tongue in a rhythm that invited, even challenged, her to participate in a similar dance at another touch point of their bodies. When the fire between them burned out of control, he grasped her panties and pushed them down over her hips. When he couldn't reach to get them all the way off, he trailed kisses down her body. She was completely naked by this time, and he didn't return to kiss her mouth. Instead, she felt his tongue against her inner thigh, urging her to yield.

Her control vanished as he stroked the sensitive skin again and again until she was certain she would explode with her own passion. She pulled at him desperately until he covered the length of her with his own body. She opened to him and felt their twin intakes of breath as he slipped in. Then he thrust into her slowly, agonizingly, until she locked her legs around his back, seeking to draw him more completely inside her.

It was everything she'd relived in her dreams and nightmares since her return to New York. The wild abandon of Joshua's lovemaking had both consoled and haunted her as she'd waited through sleepless nights for him to come back to her. Now he was here. There was no reserve, no inhibition, no thought of anyone or anything other than him and her.

He spoke her name in a whisper that built to a cry as they released the passion they'd only been able to imagine during those lost weeks.

Lulled by the rhythm of the car as it sped along the highway toward Connecticut, they lay quietly in each other's arms without words. Now they touched. They brushed away an errant curl, kissed a closed eyelid, murmured the other's name and dozed lightly. After a time Josh raised himself on one elbow and studied her, his hands never still as he lightly caressed the silhouette of her body.

"Marlo, I was saving this for the proper time—later at dinner, perhaps—but now I realize there's no way to set up such a moment. I should have told you weeks ago, when I first realized it. Maybe then you wouldn't have left. I love you, Marlo, and I want to marry you."

She lay very still. While she'd known they loved each other even in the midst of their separation, she was unprepared for him to propose marriage. For all his abandon in making love, Joshua still had a strong practical side. She knew from watching him during the months they'd worked together that he thought through every detail until he was sure that there'd be no problems. A marriage between him and Marlo was practically tripping over itself with loose ends.

When she didn't answer him right away and gazed at him with perplexity, Josh was confused. "Surely you must have known, even before I did. You always know things before I do—even about how I feel. You must've known I was in love with you since that day in the window when you were building that sexy lingerie display."

She smiled. "You mean when you nearly knocked me off that ladder, you weren't trying to get rid of me? That was a love tap?"

"I did not knock you off any ladder. I tried to catch you, as I recall," he replied with a hint of indignation she could tell he didn't mean.

"I love you, too, Josh," she said, catching him off guard as always by changing the subject when he least expected it.

"But?"

"But you know very well we have things to work out before we can talk about marriage," she said, and watched his eyes for a reaction. She saw agreement there, grudging as it was.

The intercom buzzed and Josh picked it up, muttered, "Thank you, James," and hung up. "We'll discuss this over dinner. James tells me we're within thirty minutes of the inn. Perhaps we should get dressed." He leaned in for a quick kiss on her stomach and then began to untangle their clothing.

# Ten

———

When they reached the inn, James drove around to a small cottage overlooking a lake and unloaded two suitcases. Inside waited a cozy dinner for two, complete with candlelight and cold shrimp salads with fresh fruit. Josh regaled Marlo with stories of how he'd gotten Gordon Madison and her building super to cooperate with his plans.

"He actually let you into the apartment to pack a suitcase for me?" Marlo was astonished.

Josh smiled. "Just think, if only your burglars had known that all they had to do was give the super fifty dollars to unlock the front door...."

Marlo was steaming. "I'm going to write the landlord such a letter," she threatened, then gulped down her wine.

"Well, maybe the guy has a soft streak. I told him it was all in the interest of romance." Josh shrugged and reached across the table to feed her a plump strawberry. "What do you expect? It's spring, and as Patrick pointed out to me just the other day, the world tends to fall in love with love in April."

"Patrick was in on this, too?" She was beginning to think everyone had known but her.

"Not exactly. Actually, he thought my timing wasn't very original. He's prepared to stage a protest if we dare to set the wedding date in such a conventional month as June. I was thinking we could fool them all and get married sooner—like tomorrow?"

Marlo glanced at him, expecting to see the familiar teasing glint in his eyes, but he was not only serious but hopeful. "Well?" he said softly.

"Joshua, I'm convinced that you have a good streak of fun and adventure in you. You don't have to keep this up any longer."

"I'm not trying to convince you I can be spontaneous," he said. "I'm trying to ask you again to marry me. I'm still waiting for an answer."

"It's the most tempting question anyone has ever asked me, Josh, but we have so many things to work out first—"

His fork hit the china plate with a clatter before she could go on. "Dammit, woman, when did we change places? I'm supposed to be the cautious conservative. Your role is that of the uninhibited radical, remember?"

"Look me straight in the eye and tell me you could accept my work as part of our life together. Tell me that you're willing to accept the facts that you have your career and I have mine and the two are not necessarily compatible. Tell me that somewhere deep inside, you aren't secretly hoping that after we're married I'll be happy to become involved with the store and leave my designing to the community theater now and then."

"I know how important your career is to you," Josh admitted grudgingly.

"But?"

"But I can't deny that I think there have to be priorities."

"Meaning that in your view my priorities should be our life together, first at any cost, while my career adapts itself to that? What about your priorities? Are you going to tell me that some of the time Carrington's won't come first when we're married?"

"Carrington's will be our livelihood—sometimes it will have to come first in order for us to survive." Josh bit off the words as he attacked his dessert.

"And sometimes," Marlo said quietly after several moments of uneasy silence, "my work will have to come first in order for me to survive as an individual—as the person you've asked to marry you."

When he didn't reply, Marlo picked at her own dessert and sipped her coffee. Josh was very quiet, as if he needed the silence to wrestle with whatever he would say next. A couple of times she saw him raise his head and study her and even open his mouth to say something. But then he would close off the comment and turn to stare again out the bay window.

Always unable to endure a silent battle, Marlo cleared the table, then set the tray of dishes outside the door of the cottage and came to stand behind Josh, snaking her arms around his waist to draw him close to her. "Joshua, let's not spoil your lovely surprise. I love you and you love me—surely we can start with that."

She felt some of the tension leave him, and he turned and held her for a long moment. "Let's go for a walk," he suggested, finally breaking his silence with a kiss on the top of her head.

"If we *were* to get married," Josh said as they strolled along the shore of the small lake, "and we could live anywhere in the world, where would you choose?"

"Probably Milwaukee," Marlo answered, and saw his surprise. "Well, it is the most practical, don't you think?" She grinned up at him.

"I've created a monster," he groaned. "Just a few short months ago a beautiful, whimsical Peter Pan stepped into my life, and single-handedly I've turned her into a raving conservative."

"I am not a conservative," she protested, rapping his arm playfully with her small fist.

For several minutes they walked in a comfortable silence. "What about children?" he asked.

"I give up. What about children?"

"How many would you want—or would you want any at all?" She couldn't read his expression in the darkness, but she sensed that he had a lot riding on her answer.

"Three, maybe four. How about you?"

"I've never really thought about it," he mused, "until now. Four sounds like a lot."

Marlo giggled. "Not when you're from a house of seven."

"Seven?" She could hear the clear amazement in his voice. "You told me you had brothers and sisters, but seven? Your mother must have had her hands full day and night."

"Things could get pretty hectic," Marlo agreed, remembering the mad dash in the mornings to get nine people dressed, fed and out the door for school and work. "But we all made it out alive."

"It must have been great having your mom there when you all came home from school," Josh said almost to himself, and suddenly Marlo saw the fantasy he was painting of her childhood.

"Josh, my mother has always had a job, and if you and I get married, our lives and those of our children we may have will flow into one another. Sometimes I won't be physically there and you'll have to be. Other times that will reverse. But you'll know and I'll know and our children will know that being there for one another has very little to do with physically being in the same room or building. There are families that spend nearly twenty-four hours a day together and might as well live on different continents."

"Being together in the traditional sense of a family is very important to me," he said stubbornly. "I'm not saying that I didn't have a good childhood or that I wasn't loved. But I am saying that for my family I want more—better."

"And what makes you think we can't have that?" she challenged him.

"It's not that I don't think we can. It's more that I think it may take more..." His words trailed off as if he were reluctant to finish the thought.

"More than I'm willing to give?" she finished for him. "Well, let me tell you something, Mr. Joshua Carrington the third, if there is going to be a Joshua *Fletcher* Carrington the fourth, then it's going to take more than just his *mother* making compromises." She stalked ahead of him, her anger evident in the firm posture of her body and the haughty tilt of her head.

"I know that," he said, catching up with her and matching his stride to hers. "Look, I'm a little spoiled. Okay." He grinned sheepishly and held up his hands in surrender. "I'm a lot spoiled. But I'm a quick study, don't you think?"

He was trying to recapture the mood of their earlier ride to the cottage, and because Marlo wanted that as well, she capitulated and smiled back at him. Hooking her arm through his, she turned back toward their cottage. "Come on, Carrington, let's get some sleep."

When they'd spent every day and night together in the mansion in Milwaukee, Josh had started a trivia game designed to let them get to know each other better. He called it "Favorites," telling her the idea had come from a movie he'd seen.

"Favorite song," he would say in the middle of dinner or a quiet evening when they were both preoccupied by work.

"Anything by the Beatles," she'd answered. "My turn. Favorite politician."

"Bobby Kennedy," he'd replied, and then laughed at her shock. "You were thinking some right-wing conservative, weren't you?"

Now as they lay together in the large, quilt-covered bed in the cottage, Josh picked up the game on a more personal note. "Favorite birthday party," he said softly as he held her cradled against him and they listened to the sounds of the night in the country.

"That's a toughie," Marlo answered, half asleep. And then suddenly she sat up, wide awake. "Oh, no," she moaned. "I forgot all about it."

"What is it?" Josh sat up also, instantly alarmed.

"My sister Jessica's fortieth-birthday party—it's tomorrow. The whole clan's going to be home. I can't be the only one not there."

"What time and where?"

"Major birthdays in our family tend to be like the stereotypical Irish wake or Polish wedding. They go on for days. Those who are on Long Island have probably already started tonight. The rest will gather there all day tomorrow, and the party will probably run through the weekend."

"Could you bring a guest?" Josh asked the question so shyly that Marlo had to smile.

"Of course. You mean you wouldn't mind going? You have no idea what you're in for," she warned him. "We're talking about eight more of me, plus assorted in-laws and nieces and nephews...."

"Sounds like fun," he laughed, pulling her back to burrow with him deep under the covers. "We'll get an early start in the morning and swing by your apartment so you can pick up anything you might need."

"I don't think you have any idea what you're agreeing to," Marlo muttered against his kisses.

"Afraid I won't measure up?" he teased her.

"Nope. I'm afraid you'll run screaming into the night, thankful to have escaped with your bachelorhood intact."

"Not a chance. I plan to organize the troops to support me in my campaign to get you to the altar as soon as possible."

"You're crazy, Joshua Carrington," Marlo laughed.

"Ah, music to my ears." He grinned and kissed her into silence.

The Fletcher home was on a tree-lined street that seemed as far removed from Manhattan as Milwaukee was. It was a large white frame house with a wide side porch and a spacious yard with budding tulips, and daffodils nodding merrily in the April breeze. Josh didn't know what he'd expected, but he knew this particular bit of Americana wasn't it.

As he and Marlo walked up the brick path to the door, he was surprised to see the front of the house draped in black and shocked to notice what was clearly a funeral wreath hanging next to the door. He turned with great concern to Marlo, whom he expected to be in a state of shock at seeing such trappings of grief, when what she'd expected was a party. What could've gone wrong?

"Marlo, I'm sorry. . ." he began, and then stopped in his tracks as the woman he loved burst into convulsive laughter.

"I love it!" she gasped between belly howls. Clearly the woman was in shock.

"Marlo." He pulled her firmly into the circle of his arms, trying simultaneously to comfort her and to protect her from the prying eyes of neighbors, who might mistake her behavior for anything other than distress. But one neighbor, working in his flower beds next door, looked up with a wide grin and gave a cheery greeting to the hysterical Marlo.

"Marlo!" Josh demanded, shaking her in an effort to bring her back to her senses. Tears were running down her cheeks, and he was suddenly taken with her vulnerability. "Oh, Marlo," he whispered, and tried to draw her close again.

"Joshua." She was trying to talk but simply offered him a black-bordered vellum card she'd removed from the stack on a small table near the front door. She wiped her eyes as he read aloud the inscription on the engraved card:

Please respect the mourning and grief of this house at the passing into middle age of our dear daughter Jessica. Her *much younger* brothers and sisters regret to announce her passage into that time of life known as 'over-the-hill' and request your cooperation in making Jessica as comfortable as possible with her new status.

"That's macabre," Josh whispered as Marlo composed her face into a serious mask of grief and prepared to lift the door knocker.

"Nope," she replied gaily. "That's my family."

"Good afternoon, Miss Marlo." A somber, gray-haired man answered Marlo's knock. He embraced Marlo and then handed her a ridiculous black sequined hat with a veil that just covered her eyes.

"Martin," Marlo replied, trying to keep from bursting into renewed giggles. "This is Josh Carrington. Josh, this is my brother-in-law Martin, husband of the bereaved Jessica." She couldn't contain herself a minute longer and doubled over in fresh gales of laughter. "Martin," she gasped as she grinned up at him. "This is terrific!"

"It is a great idea, isn't it?" Martin seemed quite pleased about the whole party. "Wait till you see the decorations." With that, he led the way down a hall to the rear of the house.

A brightly lit sun-room off a spacious family room looked out over the large backyard. The windows were all draped in black crepe, and scattered around the room were bouquets of white daisies in black vases. Someone pressed a glass of champagne and a black-bordered napkin that read "Over the Hill" into Josh's hand and then turned to hug Marlo. "Well, little sister, it's about time you got here."

"Josh, my brother Danny. And this is Tom. And over there is Vicki." Marlo waved at a striking brunette across the room. Marlo's voice was high with excitement, and there were several people converging on her and Josh to collect hugs and kisses. It was overpowering. "Hi, Mom, we made it," she said, hugging a graying version of herself who was dressed in a flowing black caftan, her hair wrapped in a white satin turban. She was forced to throw the introduction over her shoulder as she was led away by Jessica.

"Well, Josh, welcome."

Josh offered his hand and what he hoped was a normal smile, but Marlo's mother ignored both and reached up to give him a hug as exuberant as the one she'd just shared with her daughter. "I certainly hope you've arrived to make up for all the wasted time you and Marlo had been punishing yourselves with by staying apart. Life's too short, you know." Josh could see where Marlo got her candor.

"Ham, come over here and meet Marlo's Joshua," Marlo's mother called to a balding man who had the face of Santa Claus minus the beard. It occurred to Josh that these people were going to be wonderful grandparents.

"Ham?" This time Josh made sure his offered handshake was accepted, but he couldn't control the question mark at the man's name.

"Hamilton Fletcher. Marlo's father. It's good to finally meet you after all this time. We were beginning to think Marlo had made you up just to keep Vicki on her toes." The man had a wonderful laugh that seemed to start somewhere around his knees and then rumble its way up and out. "Have you met the whole clan?" And before Josh could say another word, the older man had taken him firmly in hand and was ushering him around, introducing him as "Marlo's beau."

When they'd completed their circuit of the room, the one thing Josh had learned was that everyone in the room was a relative. There were brothers and sisters and their spouses, as well as nieces and nephews of all ages plus grandparents. "Lucy, you'd better get the man something a bit stronger than this watered-down punch. I think he's a little overwhelmed." Ham Fletcher sounded concerned.

Lucy Fletcher gave her husband a warm look and led Josh toward the buffet. "Have you eaten yet, Josh? Perhaps you'd join me? I've been so busy preparing the feast I haven't had a chance to enjoy any of it." They filled plates, and she led Josh to two relatively secluded wing-backed chairs near the fireplace.

"I suppose we Fletchers can be a bit much if you aren't used to such large families. Marlo tells me you're an only child. In some ways that must have been very nice."

They ate and chatted, and Josh found himself relaxing despite the boisterous sounds of the party that surrounded them.

"Please don't get the idea that we're this ridiculous all the time," Lucy said as she stood to take his plate and return to the rest of her guests. "Just about sixty percent of the time." She smiled. "The rest of the time we're *very serious*." She stressed the last two words dramatically and then smiled. "I'll send Marlo to rescue you," she promised, and left him.

"So, how do you like a large family?" Marlo grinned wickedly when she reached Josh's chair.

"You deserted me," he said.

"I did it on purpose. The only way to see if you can swim on your own in the Fletcher household is to throw you in head first."

"And?"

"Not bad, kid. Not bad at all. At first I thought you were going to sink, but just when you were going down for the third time, I saw you take a deep breath and start to paddle."

"I'm glad I passed," Josh said wryly.

"Oh, you passed, all right. The room is abuzz with conversation about you—about us. Speculation is running rampant. Bets are being placed."

"Your father insisted on introducing me as your 'beau,'" Josh said, grimacing.

Marlo laughed. Then she leaned back in the large chair and happily surveyed the room. "It's great to see everyone at the same time," she sighed.

"How long has it been?" Josh, remembering the long absences of members of his own family, was immediately sympathetic.

"We were all here for Easter."

"Easter was just a couple of weeks ago," Josh said in astonishment.

"I know, but since then I've been so busy and Vicki's play opened and Dan had to be out west—well, it just seems like we've been out of touch."

"You stay in that close contact?"

"Sure. We're on the phone back and forth several times a week—you should've seen my long-distance bills while I was in Milwaukee. When we can manage, we get together for lunch or coffee."

"That's nice." Josh sounded wistful. "It's great that you all live so close."

"Well, not really." Marlo grinned. "Danny lives in Pennsylvania, and Vicki takes off for Maine every summer to do stock up there. Tom works for a senator in D.C...."

"Okay, make your point," Josh grumbled.

"My point is that it's possible to be separated for even long periods of time and still be close if you learn to work at it and plan ahead and make special times together like this one—" she gestured to include the room filled with people "—memorable."

"Vicki's little girl seems to have accepted her mother's acting career," he mused, watching the tiny version of Vicki as she moved easily through the room.

"That's mainly because Vicki has taken the time to explain to Lauren why acting is so important to her. Look, Josh, peo-

ple didn't raise their kids the same way in your mom and dad'
day. Maybe if Sally and your dad had taken the time to assur
you that when they went away they'd be back and why it wa
important to them to go away, you'd have accepted it, too
Yours was an unusual childhood, filled with people leaving and
even sometimes not coming back at all. But that's not the
norm, you know.''

"I'm beginning to see that. I'm also beginning to wonder i
you didn't stage this whole thing just to show me how wrong
could be.'' He smiled at her and watched her earnestness with
obvious pleasure.

*"Moi?"* she replied with wide-eyed innocence. "Would I g
to such extremes just to capture the man I love?''

"I certainly hope so," Josh said, and his eyes darkened with
a hint of the love and passion she aroused in him.

The party continued well into the night, with people coming
and going throughout the evening. It was an unseasonabl
warm April night, and some guests drifted out into the yard to
continue conversations and share news. Josh found himsel
deep in conversation about retailing trends with Marlo'
brother-in-law Martin. He even found the time to shoot some
baskets with her nephews, and he danced with Marlo and each
of her sisters.

When they finally called it a night, Josh was amused to se
that dormitory-style arrangements had been made for the visi
tors, with two large bedrooms set aside for the men and two fo
the women. The family room was decked out in wall-to-wal
sleeping bags for the kids. A few seconds after the lights were
finally out, he laughed out loud to hear Jessica start the famil
iar curtain call from the television show *The Waltons*.

"Good night, Mama," she called through the still house.

And Lucy answered. "Good night, Jessica. Good night
Tom."

After Tom and three or four others had answered and lou
giggles were coming from every corner of the house, Han
Fletcher ended the sequence with a booming "Good night
John Boy," that left no doubt that it was time to cut the antic
and get some sleep.

Josh lay awake for some time, listening to the silence of the house. It felt so comfortable. He liked these people, and they seemed to have taken him in, simply on the basis of his love for Marlo. He noticed that there seemed to be no doubt that the two of them would marry—in fact, he'd heard Jessica and her mother discussing plans for Marlo's shower.

It was clear that for the Fletcher family, the ideas of love, marriage and family went together. Marlo had been right all along. Life was a risk. He had no right to expect that a marriage could be planned down to the last detail, the way some business deals could. No, that wasn't quite it. Business had its risks, too—played out against the whims of a fickle public. Today the people loved the concept of Carrington's having everything they needed in one department. Tomorrow someone would build a better mousetrap or, in this case, a more innovative way of merchandising. Surely two people who loved each other as he and Marlo did had a better chance of controlling their destiny than that.

She'd told him her work was important to her beyond what it gave her. She'd said that it added to her definition as an individual and that to remove it would change her into someone she was not. Well, I don't want anyone else, Josh thought, just Marlo.

Across the hall, Marlo was having similar thoughts. She'd been delighted with the way Josh had fallen in with her family as if his place had always been there, just waiting for him to assume it. She'd had no doubt that the family would accept him, but had to admit to herself that she'd had a moment of doubt about Josh himself.

Oh, Joshua, she thought, can we make this work? Can I get you to visualize it working? Okay, Marlo, try thinking like he does—logically. What are the stumbling blocks? Your work is the only one. Marlo carried on the mental dialogue with her alter ego thinking as Josh. After several minutes of the exercise, she smiled. She had at least a part of the answer. If bringing Josh home to meet her family had erased at least some of the doubts for each of them, then maybe...

* * *

"Marlo," Josh said the following morning as he walked outside with her to fill the bird feeders that dotted the yard, "I've been thinking about us and the things we were...um, discussing up at the cottage."

"I've been thinking about that, too, and I've got a great idea, Josh."

"No, let me finish." Josh stopped her torrent of words with one finger. "I've been thinking how unfair I've been. After all, you were able to spend months seeing my work and being a part of that element of my life, while I've practically denied the fact that your career exists. A lot of that, you understand—or should I say we both understand—had to do with my own biases against the theater world in general, of course."

"Because of Sally's career?"

"That and my father's flamboyance. Somehow the two always seemed related to me. Anyway, I'm not ten any longer, waiting around for my parents to have some time for me. The point is it's time I took a look at your work, through your eyes."

Marlo's smile was dazzling.

"What?" Josh said when she couldn't seem to stop smiling.

"I had exactly the same idea last night," she said, laughing. "'Self,' I said, lying there in the dark, 'maybe if Josh could see you at work, he'd be able to understand what it means to you.' Great minds . . ." She tapped the side of her forehead.

"So we can set it up?"

"No problem."

With clearance from Gordon Madison, Marlo took Josh with her on Monday when she returned to the city to supervise construction on the sets. She was dressed in her grubbiest clothes when he arrived at her apartment, and she was glad to see he'd followed her advice to do the same. They caught a subway downtown to a warehouse where construction had been in progress for several days. The place was a beehive of activity, not unlike the store the week before the spring opening.

Within minutes of their arrival, Marlo was deep in conference with the shop manager and other construction personnel.

She'd explained to Josh on the trip out that Gordon had hired professionals to be the designers and heads of teams but that the workers were amateurs—promising theater students. Josh wandered around the large warehouse and was drawn to the wall where color renderings of the proposed sets were mounted. Next to each sketch were detailed specification sheets that gave the workers all the information they would need, in some cases right down to the type of nails and hinges to be used.

He studied the plans and recognized Marlo's no-nonsense handwriting and was amazed at her technical knowledge. He stood silently in the shadows and waited as Marlo firmly but with great finesse supervised the crew in order to accomplish just what she wanted. He saw her tangle with one temperamental young artist whose assignment was a large flat that was to carry the look of an English countryside.

"It just needs more...depth," Marlo told him with quiet authority. "I know you can do it. Perhaps..." She picked up a brush and tried some strokes with a mixture of several paints. "Is that getting there?" The artist nodded enthusiastically and offered a further suggestion. Marlo grinned and handed the brush back to him. "That's the idea," she said, and clapped him warmly on the back.

Mostly Josh watched the glow of challenge that lit her eyes. He saw how her energy was sharp and vigorous, even after the long weekend and exhausting party. In a lot of ways he saw himself and Patrick and the excitement they'd shared during the long, hard years of rebuilding Carrington's. He, too, had felt the adrenaline and knew it was a source of the high color that dotted Marlo's cheeks. He saw that for the moment she was completely engrossed in her work, having forgotten entirely about him.

When it was nearly noon, she looked up and found him watching her with a silly lopsided grin. "Omigosh," she began apologetically. "I just got so caught up. We're really working close to deadline."

"I know. It's all right. But you have to eat."

"I'm really sorry, but there's no way I can leave right now." Damn, she thought, I wanted him to see that my work wouldn't come between us, and here I am, choosing that over him the first time out.

"Well, of course you can't leave now," he said, placing a large paper bag on the table in front of her. "So I went out and got sandwiches and soda."

In answer her stomach growled loudly. The warehouse was suddenly quiet, since the rest of the crew had broken for lunch en masse. Marlo grinned, rubbing her stomach to quiet it and reaching to unpack the bag.

"Well, what do you think?" she asked, not daring to look at him.

"It's exciting," he answered. "Is it always so hectic?"

"Oh, this is calm," she answered between bites of the corned beef sandwich. "It can be a lot worse than this. I was once working on a show where—"

Her words were drowned out by a series of ear-splitting crashes on the far side of the warehouse. As they rushed to the scene, along with the rest of the crew, they saw a shambles of wood and canvas and spattered paint. Apparently one flat that'd been leaned against a support post to dry had not been properly steadied. When it had fallen, it had started a domino effect that sent other flats and scenery pieces flying, as well as open buckets of paint.

The shop manager was swearing a blue streak, but Marlo just calmly walked around, assessing the damage. With the help of Josh and those workers still in the building, she created order out of the chaos until they could tell exactly what would have to be redone. "This one," she said very quietly, almost eerily so, as far as Josh was concerned. He almost would have preferred tears and hysterics; at least then he might've known what to do. "This one we can salvage," she called out as a worker carried another broken piece of the set away. "Damn," she muttered under her breath as she surveyed the total damage and the crew gathered silently around her.

"Okay," she said after taking a deep audible breath and turning to face the young workers. "We've had a setback, but it isn't the end of the world. If we have another, *that* will be the end of the world." She grinned and ran her fingers through her short dark hair. The men and women of the crew breathed in relief and awaited instructions.

"Suffice it to say we'll have to work around the clock to get back on track, and we'll have to break up into skeleton crews so we don't go over budget. We'll split up into three crews for four five-hour shifts. That way enough of you will be able to get some rest and carry through on a regular day tomorrow."

Josh noticed that she devoted no time to pointing fingers of blame or demanding that the guilty party step forward. And there was no question that the one person who planned to be there regardless of the time was Marlo. With a couple of good-natured gibes, Marlo dismissed the crew so that they could return to work, reminding them that paint buckets commonly came with covers and that the floor or walls were far more secure resting places for drying scenery flats than skinny posts in the middle of the room.

"I'm really sorry, Josh, but it can't be helped. Do you think you can find your way back on the subway all right?"

"I'm sure I can, but why should I?"

"Josh, I know we'd planned to spend most of the evening together. I wanted that more than anything. But this—"

"I'm staying," he said quietly. "Now, tell me what I can do to help."

"That's not necessary," she stammered.

"Look, you helped me when I was in a jam. Why can't I do the same for you? I may not be a scenic artist, but I can swing a paintbrush, and I can hammer a nail or hold a board or be the best gofer you ever met. How about giving me a job, lady?"

"You're hired," Marlo said with relief. Within minutes she had introduced him to the rest of the crew as an extra pair of hands. The idea was met with enthusiastic applause. "First assignment," Marlo said with mock sternness. "Coffee, and lots of it."

"Aye-aye, Captain." He saluted her and left.

They worked through the night and into the morning. When the full crew reported at eight, Marlo sent the final skeleton shift home for some much-needed sleep. Then she came to the office to find Josh.

"Ready to go?" he asked, gathering his denim windbreaker and her sweatshirt.

"I can't leave," Marlo answered, incredulous.

"Of course you can leave. You've been here for twenty-four hours straight. You've handled the crisis brilliantly. Everything is back on schedule, and you need some rest before you drop." This was Joshua Carrington, president of a top department store, used to giving orders and used to having them obeyed without question.

"This is my project, Josh, and we're at a critical point in its development. Let me decide where I must be when and how much sleep I can do without, please." Her voice had taken on the same deadly quiet he'd noticed when the accident first happened.

"Look, honey," Josh began with a weariness that was evident in his tone and eyes.

"Don't patronize me," Marlo snapped, and shuffled some of the papers on the desk next to her.

"I'm not patronizing!" Josh shouted with exasperation. "I've been working my butt off trying to show some respect for you and your work, but this is insanity. You're ruining your health for one show. It doesn't make sense."

"I'm in fine health. Just because I'm tired doesn't mean I'm not in good health, and this one show could be a turning point for me just as the spring opening was the culmination of a dream for you. I repeat: do not patronize me."

Josh's next sound came out in an unintelligible growl as he placed his hand on the doorknob. Then he hesitated as if there was something more he wanted to say.

But before he could make up his mind to say it, Marlo began to fling words out as quickly as they came to mind, with no thought as to what they were or what damage they might inflict. "And another thing, Josh. While we all appreciate everything you did yesterday and last night, please don't ever feel obligated to make such a sacrifice again. If you aren't going to respect my work just on the basis that it's my work, then I don't need any of your grandstand plays to prove how understanding you can be."

It was all pure venom and exhaustion, and she regretted the words the minute they were out. She was terrified of losing him, irritated that she hadn't been able to show him her work calmly, instead of having to run around half the night like a crazy lady, and she was feeling a great deal sorry for herself. She heard rather than saw him turn the knob and knew that he was going without a backward look. She swallowed hard and turned to take back her outburst, to ask him for his understanding and patience, but he was gone. "Damn," she muttered again.

# Eleven

By the time everything was under control to Marlo's satisfaction, it was dark again, and she was exhausted to the point of bone-weariness. She clung to a strap in the crowded subway and felt herself being jostled and bumped by the other commuters and the motion of the train. At her stop she emerged into the street along with hundreds of other New Yorkers anxious to be home, their faces mirrors of one another, masks of weariness and stress.

Outside her apartment door, Marlo sniffed the air hungrily. Somewhere in the building a feast was being prepared, or at least it seemed that way to Marlo after two days of cold sandwiches and gallons of bitter coffee. How nice it would be to come home to a hot meal, a warm bath and someone to hold her and rub the tension from her back as she spilled out the frustrations of her day. But she had certainly seen to that, hadn't she? There would be no warm hugs waiting for her after her hysterics of the morning. Josh must be safely back in Milwaukee by now. She'd called his hotel around noon to apologize and been told he'd checked out.

Her apartment was depressingly dark. She wished she'd remembered to leave a light on so that she wouldn't have had to walk into a dark room. She flicked the switch that lit the small entry and put her portfolio and jacket in the closet. She moved into the kitchen and automatically stood before the open refrigerator, trying to decide what there was to eat that would require no preparation yet satisfy the emptiness in the pit of her stomach.

"You'll spoil your dinner that way."

Marlo jumped at the unexpected sound of Josh's voice and whirled to find him lounging against the doorjamb of her kitchen as if he'd lived there for years. His face was lined with fatigue and tension as he switched on the glaring fluorescent light and studied her closely.

"Josh." It was all she could think of to say. She'd been so certain he'd gone, following his normal pattern of leaving in the face of conflict, that she hadn't even begun to prepare the speech of apology she now needed for her irrational outburst of the morning. "Josh . . ." she tried again.

"Why don't you take a hot shower while I finish up with dinner? We can talk after we eat—when we're both in a little better shape." He walked past her without touching her and lifted the lid on her slow cooker to stir the contents. The smell that had tempted her in the hallway assaulted her senses, and she heard her stomach growl.

"All right. Go on and get in the shower and I'll bring you some cheese and crackers for an appetizer," he said, answering the sound of her stomach but not turning around to address her. There was no humor in his voice as he bent to taste his creation.

It was difficult for her to gauge his mood. On the one hand, he could be angry—certainly she'd given him every right to be. But would a man who was angry hang around an empty apartment all day, cooking, without knowing whether she'd be home to eat? No, not angry. Stern. He was very stern, the way he'd get at the store when things were going badly and he had some unpleasant decisions to make. She knew from experience that in such cases he both dreaded and anticipated getting such business settled.

The shower felt wonderful. She washed her hair and stood for several minutes under the pulsing spray, letting it vibrate against the tense muscles of her neck and back. When she stepped out of the shower, she saw through the steam that on the sink counter were a small plate of cheese and crackers and a glass of dark red wine. Marlo ate ravenously while she dressed in clean jeans and a oversize sweater.

Then, catching a glimpse of herself in the mirror, she changed her mind. This was hardly the time to look like Annie Oakley. The man she loved and wanted, more than anything, to spend the rest of her life with was in the next room—miraculous as that might seem after her totally unwarranted outburst of the morning. This was a time for femininity, for a touch of perfume and lipstick, for something that would take his attention from the dark circles beneath her eyes and pull it down to the soft curves of her body.

She stripped once again and then wrapped herself in her blue silk robe. She noted with satisfaction that there was no question that beneath the robe she was completely naked. Barefoot, she walked into the kitchen. "Thanks for the crackers. I was really famished," she said softly as she rinsed the plate and left it in the dish drainer.

"Why don't you go into the living room and put your feet up?" Josh began, not looking at her as he chopped vegetables for a salad. Then he glanced over his shoulder, and she heard him catch his breath. But he turned back to his work with a vengeance.

"Can't I help?" She moved a step closer, and he stepped away as if burned.

"I've got it," he answered tensely. "Just go take it easy. I thought we'd eat in there and watch the news."

Now it was Marlo's turn to be surprised. "The news?" He couldn't be serious. They'd barely spoken three words since she'd walked into the apartment, and they certainly had volumes to say. "You want to watch the news?" Her incredulous tone forced him to turn and face her.

"No, I want to have dinner. I want you to have your first decent meal in two days, and I want that meal to be digestible. If we sit across a dinner table from each other right now, one of two things will happen. One—we'll start to talk and end up in a fight because we're both overtired and upset, or—two—we won't talk at all and the silence will have the effect of making this fabulous stew taste like cardboard. We're watching the news.''

She knew he was right. From the moment she'd seen him standing there in her kitchen, she'd fantasized about falling into his arms and having him hold her and the two of them going to bed together and making love until they could no longer fight off the exhaustion or until dawn—whichever came first. But there was a wall around him—a wall not unlike the one she'd seen during those first weeks of working for him. It was the protective fortress he seemed capable of putting up at the least sign of a problem until he'd had the time to consider the situation and decide what to do. She had an eerie feeling that after dinner the wall would come down, because at that moment Josh Carrington seemed very determined and very much a man who'd decided on his plan of action.

Sitting in the living room with the television playing softly in the background, she considered the evening ahead. It occurred to her that his shutting her off without a word when he left the warehouse had been as much an overreaction as her own outburst to his order for her to leave work and get some rest. Of course, now he'd had all day to feed on that initial anger, while she'd been busy with the details of her work, activity that had certainly dissipated a lot of her ire. She felt at a disadvantage.

Yet he was in many ways acting out of character. She was used to him closing himself off from her, physically as well as emotionally. Hadn't he done that by taking off for the family cottage after learning of her decision to return to New York? But this time he was physically here, and from all indications, he had every intention of meeting their conflict head-on, once they'd finished dinner. Warily she accepted the plate of stew and the salad he placed on the snack table in front of her. She didn't even protest when he replaced her wineglass with one filled with milk.

He sat in a chair across the room, eating and watching the news. Only once did he look at her. That was when she com-

plimented him on the stew. He studied her for a moment, as if
unsure that she was being sincere, then nodded and resumed his
own meal. Marlo was ready to explode from the pressure of the
uncleared air she felt surrounding her. A well-digested meal
indeed.

Not even the news could distract her from the tension, which
was palpable in that living room. When they were finished, she
picked up their plates and returned them to the spotless kitchen.
Everything had been put away; the room was pure Joshua—
organized, everything in its place. Marlo sighed and returned
to the sofa, clicking the television off as she passed it.

"Okay, Josh, you're right," she began after several minutes
of watching him try to form the words he wanted to say. She sat
Buddha-style on the sofa, her hand holding the fabric of the
robe to conceal her nakedness. Suddenly the try at seduction
seemed silly, and she wished she'd stuck with the jeans and
sweater. "It won't work."

There, she'd gotten out the words she was certain he was
struggling to say. The snap of his head as he looked directly at
her confirmed it. He must have been working on his exit speech
all day, she thought. How like Josh to want to make a clean
break, with no untidy loose ends. And to do that, he'd forced
himself to stay when all he really wanted to do was get out of
there. She was positive that was the case. Yet because he loved
her, he'd stayed, probably thinking that to do so would cause
the minimum of hurt. And because she loved him, she decided
to make it easier for him.

"I guess it's pretty clear," she said, fighting to keep the
words positive even as she lied. "I mean, we've known from the
beginning how different our worlds are. It was just fantasy to
imagine we might ever be able to pull it off." She tried a laugh
but recognized it as a choke. She swallowed hard and tried
again. "If ever there were two mismatched people in the
world..." Tears had started to roll down her cheeks. "Oh,
Josh," she moaned miserably, "I don't want to lose you."

"You've always talked too much, Marlo," he said huskily,
and moved to offer her a clean handkerchief. While she composed herself, he paced the room. "Better?" he asked after
several minutes, and she nodded. He resumed his pacing.

"Marlo, a long time ago I created a dream of what a real family would be like. What it would be like to be married and have children and make a home. I realize that I set out to fill in the blanks on that fantasy exactly the way I first dreamed it. I created a mold, and I went looking for someone to fill it."

"And I can," Marlo said passionately. "You'll see. I can change. You saw me at my absolute worst today. I was nervous about the show and you, and...I can come back with you. Gordon can get somebody else. I'll even work at the store. I can be happy with community theater—some community groups are almost professional." She heard the desperation in her voice and knew that she was lying to him as well as to herself. She loved him so much that the thought of the pain she would have to endure when he left her was almost unbearable. In that moment she would have said anything to postpone that particular agony.

"No." His tone brooked no argument as he stood looking at her. He opened his mouth to speak and then swallowed the words with a growl and ran his fingers through his hair. "I don't want your changes, Marlo. I've learned that love isn't about fitting either party into a mold as I once thought. It's about giving both people the freedom and the right to be individual and unique. I was thinking a lot about my parents today and how much Mom gave to my father. He was so insecure, so anxious to take the place of his older brother in J.P.'s heart and so terrified of failure on any level. But when he was with Mother, he was different, in everything from the way he walked to the way he dealt with people. He... God, I'm so bad at this."

Marlo was totally confused. First, he was talking about not wanting her to change for him, and then he was talking about his father. What was he trying to say? "Josh, I want to understand. You're probably the most principled man I've ever known—in your work and in the way you deal with people. All I'm saying is that I want to try to live up to that ideal."

"Dammit, woman, why can't you listen to what I'm saying! You *are* the ideal. What more ideal partner could one have in life than the person who makes you complete, who takes the best parts of you and makes them blossom, who takes the worst of you and makes it okay?" He was practically shouting.

"So what do you want, Josh?" Her own voice was rising in frustration. She'd prepared herself for farewell. This didn't sound like a farewell, but if it wasn't goodbye, then she wasn't sure what it was.

"I want you to finish this show. In the meantime, I want you to apply to every professional company within a hundred miles of Milwaukee for a resident designer's job or at least a guest spot. I want you to marry me and find a home for us. I want—I need you to keep on loving me in spite of my occasional selfishness and chauvinism and warped views about what a conventional marriage is."

"And what if there's no design opening in the area?" she asked quietly. Her heart paused as she watched him shove his hands deep in the back pockets of his jeans and stand, not facing her but staring out the window of her apartment.

"Then I want you to find a job *not* in the area where you can do some guest-designing for the coming season."

"A guest-designing job would mean being away from you," she reminded him. "Perhaps for a couple of months."

"I know." He turned and came back to sit beside her on the sofa, pulling her hands into his. "Marlo, don't ask me to pretend I'd like that—it would be awful. But I think I understand that any love that can't survive a few weeks apart is in trouble to begin with. There's just one promise I want you to make."

"What?" She asked, studying his face in search of any clue to what his final compromise might be.

"Could you start by applying to cities where they have good fashion centers, like L.A. and Dallas and Atlanta? At least then I'd have an excuse to come along for part of your stay." His eyes danced with humor.

"Do you really need an excuse?" she asked as a smile began to fight its way through the relief that was surging through her.

"Not really," he replied, pulling her fully into his arms. "But it might look better at the store."

Marlo laughed. "And how will J.P. feel about your marrying an employee?"

"Former employee. My future wife has her own career. Besides, J.P. will love it. In fact, he'll probably demand to know what the hell took so long. Is that a yes?"

"Is what a yes?"

"Are we getting married?"

"Josh Carrington, you have just put me through the most tortured evening of my life. I was ready to promise you anything—"

"Ah, but were you ready to deliver?"

"Well, not all of it. I figured there would be time to work out the details once I was certain you weren't leaving again."

"So you were lying through your teeth, weren't you? Somehow I thought the switch from independent career person to obedient hausfrau was a bit sudden."

She snuggled closer into his embrace. "Smart man. And since you failed to get any of those rash promises in writing, I guess I can safely accept your proposal—as long as we understand there are no rules."

"No rules except one. I love you, Marlo, and I intend to let you know that every day of our lives," he whispered, and gave her a kiss that said far more than his faltering words ever could. "You need some rest," he said when they finally drew apart.

"Are you taking it as your spousal right to tell me what I need and do not need?" she teased him, putting to rest the battle of the morning.

"I'm sure going to try," he growled, and carried her to the large chair so that he could unfold her sofa bed.

"I might have my own ideas about that," she whispered when he reclaimed her and carried her to bed. She outlined the silhouette of his ear with her tongue.

"Cut that out," he ordered her. "You need your rest."

"What I need is you," she answered, and pulled him off balance to topple onto the bed with her.

Their lovemaking was tumultuous and filled with passion. Finally they both slept, their arms and legs entwined, their faces devoid of the tensions that had racked them for the last twenty-four hours. Their sleep was so peaceful and deep that neither of them heard the phone when it rang somewhere around midnight. Nor did they hear the message that wound its way onto Marlo's answering machine:

"Marlo? Gordon. Josh's mother called today with a message for you. The Rep in Milwaukee is on the verge of getting

some serious money to start a third theater in their new facil-
ity. They'll be needing a full and separate staff, including a se
designer. I trust you'll let me know when and where to send the
letter of reference—as well as the wedding present? Swee
dreams, kid.''

*     *     *     *     *

*... and now an exciting short story
from Silhouette Books.*

\*

## HEATHER GRAHAM POZZESSERE

# Shadows on the Nile

### CHAPTER ONE

Alex could tell that the woman was very nervous. Her fingers were wound tightly about the arm rests, and she had been staring straight ahead since the flight began. Who was she? Why was she flying alone? Why to Egypt? She was a small woman, fine-boned, with classical features and porcelain skin. Her hair was golden blond, and she had blue-gray eyes that were slightly tilted at the corners, giving her a sensual and exotic appeal.

And she smelled divine. He had been sitting there, glancing through the flight magazine, and her scent had reached him, filling him like something rushing through his bloodstream, and before he had looked at her he had known that she would be beautiful.

John was frowning at him. His gaze clearly said that this was not the time for Alex to become interested in a woman. Alex lowered his head, grinning. Nuts to John. He was the one who had made the reservations so late that there was already another passenger between them in their row. Alex couldn't have remained silent anyway; he was certain that he could ease the flight for her. Besides, he had to know her name, had to see if her eyes would turn silver when she smiled. Even though he should, he couldn't ignore her.

"Alex," John said warningly.

Maybe John was wrong, Alex thought. Maybe this was precisely the right time for him to get involved. A woman would be the perfect shield, in case anyone was interested in his business in Cairo.

The two men should have been sitting next to each other, Jillian decided. She didn't know why she had wound up sandwiched between the two of them, but she couldn't do a thing about it. Frankly, she was far too nervous to do much of anything.

"It's really not so bad," a voice said sympathetically. It came from her right. It was the younger of the two men, the one next to the window. "How about a drink? That might help."

Jillian took a deep, steadying breath, then managed to answer. "Yes . . . please. Thank you."

His fingers curled over hers. Long, very strong fingers, nicely tanned. She had noticed him when she had taken her seat—he was difficult not to notice. There was an arresting quality about him. He had a certain look: high-powered, confident, self-reliant. He was medium tall and medium built, with shoulders that nicely filled out his suit jacket, dark brown eyes, and sandy hair that seemed to defy any effort at combing it. And he had a wonderful voice, deep and compelling. It broke through her fear and actually soothed her. Or perhaps it was the warmth of his hand over hers that did it.

"Your first trip to Egypt?" he asked. She managed a brief nod, but was saved from having to comment when the stewardess came by. Her companion ordered her a white wine, then began to converse with her quite normally, as if unaware that her fear of flying had nearly rendered her speechless. He asked her what she did for a living, and she heard herself tell him that she was a music teacher at a junior college. He responded easily to everything she said, his voice warm and concerned each time he asked another question. She didn't think; she simply answered him, because flying had become easier the moment he touched her. She even told him that she was a widow, that her husband had been killed in a car accident four years ago, and that she was here now to fulfill a long-held dream, because she had always longed to see the pyramids, the Nile and all the ancient wonders Egypt held.

She had loved her husband, Alex thought, watching as pain briefly darkened her eyes. Her voice held a thread of sadness when she mentioned her husband's name. Out of nowhere, he wondered how it would feel to be loved by such a woman.

Alex noticed that even John was listening, commenting on things now and then. How interesting, Alex thought, looking across at his friend and associate.

The stewardess came with the wine. Alex took it for her, chatting casually with the woman as he paid. Charmer, Jillian thought ruefully. She flushed, realizing that it was his charm that had led her to tell him so much about her life.

Her fingers trembled when she took the wineglass. "I'm sorry," she murmured. "I don't really like to fly."

Alex—he had introduced himself as Alex, but without telling her his last name—laughed and said that was the understatement of the year. He pointed out the window to the clear blue sky—an omen of good things to come, he said—then assured her that the airline had an excellent safety record. His friend, the older man with the haggard, world-weary face, eventually introduced himself as John. He joked and tried to reassure her, too, and eventually their efforts paid off. Once she felt a little calmer, she offered to move, so they could converse without her in the way.

Alex tightened his fingers around hers, and she felt the startling warmth in his eyes. His gaze was appreciative and sensual, without being insulting. She felt a rush of sweet heat swirl within her, and she realized with surprise that it was excitement, that she was enjoying his company the way a woman enjoyed the company of a man who attracted her. She had thought she would never feel that way again.

"I wouldn't move for all the gold in ancient Egypt," he said with a grin, "and I doubt that John would, either." He touched her cheek. "I might lose track of you, and I don't even know your name."

"Jillian," she said, meeting his eyes. "Jillian Jacoby."

He repeated her name softly, as if to commit it to memory, then went on to talk about Cairo, the pyramids at Giza, the Valley of the Kings, and the beauty of the nights when the sun set over the desert in a riot of blazing red.

And then the plane was landing. To her amazement, the flight had ended. Once she was on solid ground again, Jillian realized that Alex knew all sorts of things about her, while she didn't know a thing about him or John—not even their full names.

They went through customs together. Jillian was immediately fascinated, in love with the colorful atmosphere of Cairo, and not at all dismayed by the waiting and the bureaucracy. When they finally reached the street she fell head over heels in love with the exotic land. The heat shimmered in the air, and taxi drivers in long burnooses lined up for fares. She could hear the soft singsong of their language, and she was thrilled to realize that the dream she had harbored for so long was finally coming true.

She didn't realize that two men had followed them from the airport to the street. Alex, however, did. He saw the men behind him, and his jaw tightened as he nodded to John to stay put and hurried after Jillian.

"Where are you staying?" he asked her.

"The Hilton," she told him, pleased at his interest. Maybe her dream was going to turn out to have some unexpected aspects.

He whistled for a taxi. Then, as the driver opened the door, Jillian looked up to find Alex staring at her. She felt...something. A fleeting magic raced along her spine, as if she knew what he was about to do. Knew, and should have protested, but couldn't.

Alex slipped his arm around her. One hand fell to her waist, the other cupped her nape, and he kissed her. His mouth was hot, his touch firm, persuasive. She was filled with heat; she trembled...and then she broke away at last, staring at him, the look in her eyes more eloquent than any words. Confused, she turned away and stepped into the taxi. As soon as she was seated she turned to stare after him, but he was already gone, a part of the crowd.

She touched her lips as the taxi sped toward the heart of the city. She shouldn't have allowed the kiss; she barely knew him. But she couldn't forget him.

She was still thinking about him when she reached the Hilton. She checked in quickly, but she was too late to acquire a guide for the day. The manager suggested that she stop by the

Kahil bazaar, not far from the hotel. She dropped her bags in her room, then took another taxi to the bazaar. Once again she was enchanted. She loved everything: the noise, the people, the donkey carts that blocked the narrow streets, the shops with their beaded entryways and beautiful wares in silver and stone, copper and brass. Old men smoking water pipes sat on mats drinking tea, while younger men shouted out their wares from stalls and doorways. Jillian began walking slowly, trying to take it all in. She was occasionally jostled, but she kept her hand on her purse and sidestepped quickly. She was just congratulating herself on her competence when she was suddenly dragged into an alley by two Arabs swaddled in burnooses.

"What—" she gasped, but then her voice suddenly fled. The alley was empty and shadowed, and night was coming. One man had a scar on his cheek, and held a long, curved knife; the other carried a switchblade.

"Where is it?" the first demanded.

"Where is what?" she asked frantically.

The one with the scar compressed his lips grimly. He set his knife against her cheek, then stroked the flat side down to her throat. She could feel the deadly coolness of the steel blade.

"Where is it? Tell me now!"

Her knees were trembling, and she tried to find the breath to speak. Suddenly she noticed a shadow emerging from the darkness behind her attackers. She gasped, stunned, as the man drew nearer. It was Alex.

Alex...silent, stealthy, his features taut and grim. Her heart seemed to stop. Had he come to her rescue? Or was he allied with her attackers, there to threaten, even destroy, her?

\* \* \* \* \*

*Watch for Chapter Two of SHADOWS ON THE NILE coming next month—only in Silhouette Intimate Moments.*

## Silhouette Intimate Moments

Starting in October...

# SHADOWS ON THE NILE

by

### Heather Graham Pozzessere

A romantic short story in six installments from best-selling author Heather Graham Pozzessere.

The first chapter of this intriguing romance will appear in all Silhouette titles published in October. The remaining five chapters will appear, one per month, in Silhouette Intimate Moments' titles for November through March '88.

Don't miss "*Shadows on the Nile*"—a special treat, coming to you in October. Only from Silhouette Books.

Be There!

IMSS-1

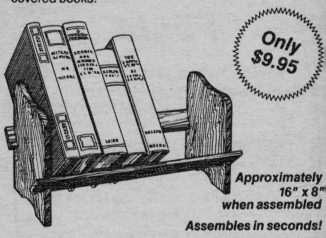

 # Silhouette Desire

## COMING
## NEXT MONTH

## AVAILABLE NOW

# In response
## to last year's outstanding success, Silhouette Brings You:

# Silhouette Christmas Stories 1987

---

Specially chosen for you in a delightful volume celebrating the holiday season, four original romantic stories written by four of your favorite Silhouette authors.

**Dixie Browning**—*Henry the Ninth*
**Ginna Gray**—*Season of Miracles*
**Linda Howard**—*Bluebird Winter*
**Diana Palmer**—*The Humbug Man*

Each of these bestselling authors will enchant you with their unforgettable stories, exuding the magic of Christmas and the wonder of falling in love.

A heartwarming Christmas gift during the holiday season...indulge yourself and give this book to a special friend!

---

## Available November 1987

XM87-